Marquel's DILEMMA

BY EMILY W. SKINNER

Edited by Ellen Williams
Cover by Sabrina of Midnight Coffee Designs on 99Designs.com
Interior Design by Lisa DeSpain

This is a work of fiction.
Any resemblance to persons living or dead is purely coincidental.

For Marquel, a beautiful, talented and loving daughter.

You bring joy and inspiration to those who are blessed to know you.

Thanks for being you. I love you, Mom.

CHAPTER ONE

1996

"I killed my husband," Joanne cried. Her ash blonde hair had grown long and formed a curtain around her face as she leaned into the palms of her hands.

"Is this a confession?" Joanne's new psychiatrist, Judith Wright, asked. Wright was a sharp 70—avid golfer and lesbian partner to 35-year-old Hollywood producer (and newly ordained minister), Greta Goldberg. While Wright was a short-statured woman with salt and pepper cropped hair, her lover was a tall, willowy, pageboy blonde.

Wright couldn't retire. She was too driven and loved helping her female client base. She had determined in the latter part of her career that she would focus on women's issues. Her small staff consisted of Allen Burke, her receptionist, and clinical psychologist Marie Judge.

"Why did you say it like that?" Joanne sat up. "Why didn't you say Joanne? Why didn't you say, is this a confession, *Joanne?*"

"Am I talking to Joanne Manning, or Joanne Jennings?" the petite doctor countered.

"You know damn well Zach is alive."

"How did you kill George?"

"He gets a first name and I don't? Why didn't you say, how did you kill your husband'"

"First names are important to you, Joanne?"

She knew Dr. Wright was speaking to her prior identity. When she was a television actress and the public knew her only by her stage name, Marquel.

"Oh, God..." She felt a wave of anxiety.

"Do you want to stop?"

She shook her head no and heaved.

"Okay, how did you kill your husband?"

She didn't answer, but instead stumbled over to the desk and grabbed her doctor's trash can, spilling the salmon and rice lunch she had consumed an hour earlier.

The doctor got up and buzzed her assistant to request he bring her patient a Sprite.

Joanne wanted to believe she had made progress. Not only was she a frequent guest on Oprah, but she had produced a documentary, "Fast Fall," about the tabloid exploitation that ultimately broke her psychogenic fugue state.

"Thank you," she took the iced beverage from Allen, the doctor's receptionist.

"Joanne, how do you feel now?" The doctor asked.

Her only response was to look at her doctor with tearful eyes.

She and Zach had just celebrated their third anniversary. His daughter Jackie would graduate high school in a few months and it was all flooding back... She wondered what it would have been like if her own Marquel had lived, and how she would handle the girl's prom years and graduation.

She knew George would be so proud of Marquel. She was daddy's girl.

"Let's continue. Joanne, how did you kill your husband?"

"I killed them both," Joanne went to the dark place that washed out all relevance of time.

She was in the woods running through the swamp. Her feet were bleeding and she was hungry and cold. She wanted a hunter to hear her, to see the bristle of the branches she stood behind and shoot her dead.

Wright got up and sat her thin 5'4" frame on the couch next to her challenging patient. She could see the beautiful sandy blonde was gone again. She snapped her fingers next to Joanne's left ear three times rapidly and Joanne came back. The doctor had developed this prompt to bring Joanne out of her memory trances.

"Is Zach here?" Joanne was calm, dabbing the tears with her fingertips, careful not to smudge her mascara.

"Your husband hasn't arrived y…"

Joanne remembered where she left off. The word husband resonated with her. "Doctor, why do I associate *husband* with George and not Zach?"

"You do not see Zach as your husband?"

"I do."

"What is your definition of husband?"

"A partner who is with you through good times and …" her voice drifted off.

"And?" Wright probed.

"Bad." Joanne finished.

"So a husband is someone who is with you during bad times?"

Joanne nodded and her eyes released a steady stream of tears. Her throat knotted in pain.

"Joanne, if you could tell George anything, right now, what would it be?"

She could barely think much less speak.

A knock came at the door and Wright ignored it.

"Joanne, you should write a letter to George."

"But that's how," her voice cracked, "that's how I killed him."

"You wrote him a letter that you believe… had something to do with his death?"

Joanne nodded again.

The doctor had been working with Joanne for more than a year, getting pieces of her story via their sessions as well as various media. Joanne's documentary didn't address the days leading up to George's death.

"My last letter was on the table when the authorities came to check on him. He had been missing for…" Joanne took several deep breaths. "I thought I was over the shame… it doesn't go away."

Wright understood shame of another kind. It would take her nearly 50 years to feel confident about her sexuality.

"It does," Wright stood. "Slowly."

CHAPTER TWO

Zach pulled into the parking lot of the professional complex where Joanne was in session. There was a small bouquet of wild flowers on the seat next to him that he had picked up, along with some fresh fruits, at an organic market near their home. He tried to surprise her on occasion. He knew the therapy sessions were stressful.

It had taken him some time to convince Joanne, but she finally agreed to a new doctor, a woman. When they married, she wanted to just talk things out as a couple. She had trusted him as her psychiatrist before they fell in love and wanted to keep working with him, but he needed help, too.

He had a shattered bride and a vengeful ex taking him on in the media. He also wanted to protect his daughter, Jackie, and keep a low profile, but his ex-wife Isabel made sure there was no chance of that.

Joanne and Zach both needed support systems to get through the challenges of her fall from fame and the media attack on their lives. Zach was often portrayed as an opportunist who seduced his beautiful—and younger—patient after her agent Ken had hired him. She was a troubled but talented starlet on the short-lived hit TV show, *Suburban Life*, known only by the singular name Marquel.

The unvarnished truth was that Zach was a lonely, middle-aged, divorced psychiatrist when "Marquel" entered his life.

Their sessions had been a mix of tears, anger, darkness and sexual tension. Loving her was the biggest risk he had taken since opening a practice in Beverly Hills. He understood the consequences, but broke his professional ethics for a second chance at love.

He was mesmerized by her. Rumors of a nervous breakdown were just surfacing in the gossip magazines and it was his job to keep her functioning. It was a constant struggle, trying to keep up with the demons that were haunting her.

The car door opened and Joanne's gorgeous smile sent his heart racing, as it always did. Its appearance had been so rare in their early days.

"Did you have a good session?" He could see her eyes were red.

Joanne picked up the flowers and kissed him sweetly on the mouth. "You always do the right thing."

He pulled her in for another kiss, this one lingering.

"I don't know what I'd do without you," her finger circled his mouth and she gave him another light kiss before buckling her seat belt. "You make everything right with the world."

He never felt this way with Isabel. His ex never had the look of love in her eyes when she spoke to him. This was the happiest he'd ever been with a woman.

"How about Mexican for dinner?" Joanne tried to leave her session behind her in Dr. Wright's office, much as she had left her lunch there. "I'm hungry."

"It's a bit early for dinner." He did everything he could to make her happy. "How about some cherries? I picked some up at the market."

"Are you telling me life is a bowl full of cherries?" She grabbed the bag from the back seat and plopped one in her mouth, spitting the pit into her hand.

"A belly full," he began, but she silenced him by placing a ripe cherry between his teeth as he waited to pull into traffic on Olympic Blvd. He pierced it to the pit and it squeezed a dark crimson down his chin. They both laughed and she licked his chin.

She offered her hand and he spit the pit into her palm.

"This isn't a good food for a white interior."

"You're right," Joanne grabbed a tissue from the glove box and placed the pits inside, dropping the bag on the floor as the Mercedes accelerated.

"Easy there," Zach warned. "You don't want bruises."

She surveyed her pink-stained fingers. "Ok, old man, I'll try to be tender with your fruit."

"*Our* fruit, Mrs. Manning."

"Yes, Mr. Manning. About that Mexican dinner… will you survive the heartburn?"

The car slowed to a stop at a red light.

"I'll do my best." He leaned in for another quick kiss.

He snapped a few pictures with his extended lens as the Mercedes drove out of sight and let the camera dangle around his neck. It was good being back on his own beat, doing the stories only he knew how to cover.

This time *she* wouldn't have the last word. He'd see to that.

Mark Collins had dyed his hair black and was no longer the lean, hungry reporter he once was. He had survived abduction and servitude in the jungles of South America and wanted nothing more than to offer payback to those who sent him to Colombia.

Collins' prior ill fate had been phoned-in by Zach Manning, who had "requested" via his friend Lou Bartalow that Collins end his stalking of Joanne. Zach wanted her to have a chance to recover after Collins had mercilessly published the details of her private life—details the rogue reporter obtained through a series of illegal wiretaps. Joanne was fragile and suicidal as a result and had left Zach to return to Florida with her estranged husband, George.

It happened that both Zach and Carlos Vasquez had called on Lou Bartalow for a favor, so Bartalow merely recommended Mark Collins to his friend Carlos. Then he tipped Collins off in an anonymous call, telling him that an Oscar-winning actor was buying drugs outside of Ralph's Grocery store in Long Beach. That was the setup.

Still high on having just outed Marquel's true identity and greedy for what could be another great expose, Collins never questioned the source. It was like leading a baby to a bottle. Collins would meet his informant Mr. X outside a Ralph's shortly before closing and ahead of the actor making his pickup.

Collins remembered little after leaning into the informant's van, other than a black hood being placed over his head and a blunt object making contact with his skull.

This was his initiation into the Bogotá cartel run by drug lord Carlos Vasquez.

Vasquez loved American tabloids and television and had sought out Bartalow's input regarding someone to assist him with his memoirs. The egotistical trafficker had terminal cancer and wanted the world to know his true legacy. From living on the streets as a child to becoming a rich businessman, Vasquez saw the drug trade as a supply to meet a growing demand and law enforcement as prohibition officers.

Vasquez appreciated the U.S. government's extreme generosity toward the drug dealing community. By keeping drugs illegal, only the strongest crime families survived. By keeping drugs illegal, the cartel didn't have to pay U.S. taxes or be regulated. By keeping drugs illegal, American tax dollars were spent putting drug users, American citizens, in jails where they became unproductive caged animals. The lesson was, buy drugs, make the cartel rich and if you get caught, at least you'll be sheltered, fed and clothed—albeit in a maximum security prison.

Bartalow and Vasquez met at a junket for up-and-coming filmmakers in Rio and both were intrigued with Robert Rodriquez. They formed a typical Hollywood friendship. They were each looking for a producing opportunity and a chance to discover someone and hitch their ride on the Hollywood Walk of Fame.

Vasquez was intrigued with Bartalow's selection of Mark Collins as his personal scribe. Vasquez and his posse often watched both Spanish and English language soap operas via satellite in his plush compound. Many were fans of *Suburban Life*—or *La Vida Suburbana*—as it was known in Colombia.

Collins only learned of the Bartalow friendship after he was in Bogotá for six months and finally started the Vasquez interviews. Collins knew Manning and Bartalow were friends from covering Marquel and he felt there had to be a connection in his abduction.

Vasquez loved hearing Collins' stories about stalking celebrities for *Pursuit* and he developed a kinship with the younger man. They both hungered to rise above their humble beginnings and make a name for themselves, no matter the cost.

But Collins didn't agree with Vasquez's definition. He wasn't taking people against their will.

Not surprisingly, Vasquez disagreed. He felt Collins held his victims hostage in the media. They were equals in that respect, and he was giving Collins a chance to do his "finest work".

Collins was cautious not to show his disgust for Marquel as Vasquez would hang on every word of his stories. When Collins revealed her real name, Joanne, he learned that small vigils were held in pockets of South America where telenovela fans gathered. The lines between reality and television were blurred as fans wanted to believe in "Marquel".

Collins hated Vasquez, but not as much as he hated Joanne and Zach.

At least the cartel treated him as a member of the family and eventually ranked Collins with the *lugartenientes,* the 2nd highest rank in the Vasquez family. A *lugartenientes,* or lieutenant, had priority seating at Vasquez's affairs, including weddings, baptisms, first communions, and funerals.

When Carlos Vasquez died a few years later, Collins was given a blessing by Humberto Vasquez, Carlos' eldest son, and allowed to return to the U.S. Humberto was honored by the care and quality of Collins writing. He considered the reporter a brother and vowed to help him in time of need.

The "autobiography" was released in South America titled simply as *Vasquez* in gold raised vertical lettering on the cover. The dying drug lord chose his own design. He wanted it bold as he was.

The book made its way into other markets repackaged as a biography with a pseudonym so the earnings would go to an offshore trust. This was the most legal activity the family engaged in. Mark Collins name was never tied to the book.

Law enforcement, lawyers and judges read the book for confessions, messages or curiosity regarding the minds of drug traffickers. The book made the nonfiction bestseller list and was a commercial success.

Collins kicked his motorcycle on and zipped up his leather jacket, securing the camera in place. The bike was fast, and the jacket, he was sure, hid the extra pounds he had packed on during his sedentary days in the compound. But he wasn't concerned with catching up to the Mercedes today. There would be plenty of other times to follow Zach and Joanne, and he had plenty to do before he would strike.

CHAPTER THREE

Jackie heard the garage door open and met Joanne and her father inside the garage.

"I need to borrow the car, please," Jackie kissed her father on the cheek. "You really should buy me a car."

"Is that a bribe?" He touched his cheek as she took the keys from his other hand. "If you had a car, I'd never see you."

"That's not true," Jackie was already climbing into the driver's seat.

"We'll walk to the Mexican restaurant," Zach shrugged to Joanne.

Jackie paused, not yet shutting the door, "Can you get me a burrito and save it?"

"Join us," Joanne suggested.

"Can't, I have to help Marnie with some homework and then we're going to a football game with friends." The lean 17-year old brunette started the car, quickly shutting the door.

Zach knocked on the window.

She let it down.

"Buckle up," he urged. "I can't be there to remind you all the time and you never have to give me another gift if you promise me you'll do this each time you get into a car."

Joanne's eyes welled up and Jackie felt a pang of guilt, knowing Marquel's story. She buckled her seat belt and blew a kiss to both of them as she put the electric window up.

Zach stepped back, putting an arm around Joanne's waist. "She's fearless. Makes me nervous."

Joanne's smile was a sad acknowledgment, another moment that was tough to swallow.

There was no reason for them to walk on eggshells. Their knowledge of the price she paid for her carelessness would hopefully save someone else.

CHAPTER FOUR

Lou was pissed.

Everything had been going great. It seemed he could do no wrong. Most of his business ventures were showing great returns and he and his wife were expecting their third child. He couldn't be happier... until he got the call.

He hated failure.

HATED it!

Lou Bartalow never wanted to let anyone down and he prided himself on creative solutions. Every problem could be solved with a little imagination. That was his credo.

He threw the decorative boomerang on his desk in a fury. "Son of ..."

The object flew back at him and hit the wall behind him.

Zach drove a little wildly back to the clubhouse, swerving and laughing. He and Lou had a great afternoon just knocking back a few cold ones and shooting some balls.

"Whoa Zach, you almost tossed me there," Lou was holding on to the golf cart.

"Trying to keep you on your game, Lou."

"Speaking of your game..."

"One of my best!"

"I need to tell you something," Lou motioned for him to stop.

"Before you do, I want to say thank you." Zach braked a little harder than necessary, bringing the cart to a perfunctory stop and shaking Lou's conviction in the process. "Seems like the only time we get together anymore is when our wives have a party or function where we have to put on a tux. God it was great just to get outside."

He took a deep breath and removed his sunglasses, turning to give Lou his full attention.

Lou shut his eyes and pinched the bridge of his nose. "You really know how to make a guy feel like shit."

"No Lou, I'm guilty too. I should call you more."

"I got you out here today for a reason," Lou lamented.

"An investment…" Zach laughed. "Spill it."

Lou wished he had good news to counter the bad. "He's back."

"Who's back?"

"Collins."

Zach turned, staring off at the greens.

Lou hated this. "I'm sorry," he got out of the cart, "I really figured the cartel would have killed him by now."

"Where are you going?" Zach got up and grabbed Lou's arm. "You blurt this out and walk away?"

"We're a few feet from the clubhouse. I figured I'd walk."

"You'd walk?"

"Not like that."

"Why do I get this after shooting a 77?"

"Great game by the way, Zach."

"Fuck you, Lou." Zach grit his teeth and put his sunglasses back on. He wanted to punch Lou right now. "You couldn't have just told me on the phone when we were arranging a round?"

"Do you think you would've shot a 77 if I told you before now?"

"You wanted to golf that bad?"

"No, I wanted to be a friend."

"Fuck you! I've got a problem with all of this, Lou."

Lou knew he would. "You're getting loud. Let's have a drink."

Zach got back in the cart. "Do I need to be concerned?"

Lou nodded to a few golfers walking by, waiting for them to pass. "I don't know. He was living the cartel life since he left."

Zach put his head on the steering wheel. "Jesus, Lou."

"Maybe he found Jesus."

"Living the cartel life?"

"Religion is very big in those parts, but you have a point."

"You said he wasn't coming back."

"Zach, I did what I could."

Zach raised his head, looking Lou in the eye. "What is the definition of not coming back?"

Lou stepped back. "You're fucked up."

"I'm fucked up. I'm fucked up? You just said you figured the cartel would have killed him by now."

"Well... the guy is a dick and I just thought after awhile Collins would piss Vasquez off and, you know, nail his own coffin shut."

Zach stood, moving closer to Lou. "I have to protect her. You said he wasn't coming back."

Lou nodded to a few people who were staring out the club-house window at them. "Sore loser," he mouthed and pointed at Zach.

Zach wanted to knock Lou out, but caught sight of a passing colleague. He nodded a hello as he and Lou made nice for the sake of appearances.

"Whatever you thought, Zach," Lou's voice was quiet, "you were wrong. I don't do that."

Zach had never anticipated Collins returning.

Had he asked for a hit? Was he okay assuming Lou had Collins taken out?

What kind of man did that make him? Why was this happening *now*?

His chest tightened. He knew his blood pressure was soaring.

"I love her so much." Zach muttered.

"I just wanted you to be aware," Lou patted him on the back. "Don't stress."

CHAPTER FIVE

Isabel Manning called for Carmen to answer the door.
"Did you hear the bell?" She tossed her New York Times cross-word puzzle on the glass end table.

The maid muttered in her native Spanish followed by, "Yes, Meez Ez'abel."

The doorbell continued and finally it got the best of Isabel. She left the den in a huff.

She moved quickly past the casual Carmen and picked up speed, heels clicking through the long hall and opened the door in fury.

Cameras flashed in Isabel's face. She slammed the door shut. "What's going on?"

Carmen was keenly aware that her boss was now going to hold her captive for the evening and she desperately wanted to start her weekend.

"It's the media, Carmen! Quickly, get the TV on. We need to see what's happening."

"We...' Carmen nodded and muttered more Spanish under her breath.

As Carmen moved to the kitchen, Isabel grabbed a cordless phone nearby and called Zach, who surprised her by answering on the first ring.

"Manning resid…"

He was verbally assaulted before he could complete his sentence. "Why is the media at my door?"

"Isabel?"

"I need answers!"

Carmen turned on the kitchen TV.

"Carmen! Pull the drapes. They are taking pictures of me." Isabel snapped her fingers at the maid. "What's going on? Am I supposed to be upset or happy?"

"Izzy, I have no clue." Now was not the time. He hadn't even talked with Joanne.

"Carmen change the channel!" Isabel motioned though control of the kitchen TV was well within her reach.

Carmen moved away from the curtain and tried to meet each command.

"We're not finding anything," Isabel said as she watched Carmen turn the dial of the older TV.

"No one has contacted us, Izzy."

"Well, I want Jackie to move back in with me. If there is another witch hunt for that woman, Jackie doesn't need to be exposed."

"That woman has a name. *Joanne.* They're at your door, not ours," Zach wanted to hang up, but he couldn't figure out why Isabel was the object of the press. He had to assume Collins' assault was beginning.

"*Joanne* is your wife, but I'm Jackie's mother," Isabel screeched. She knew she'd regret having given Zach primary custody of Jackie when she took a year in southern France. It seemed reasonable at the time to escape the press after Joanne's story hit. Jackie didn't want her father to be alone and begged Isabel to let her stay with him. Isabel didn't know that Joanne would eventually return or she would never have agreed.

"Call Lyle if you need someone to comfort you. That's not a high-schooler's job."

Isabel hated when he was being Mr. Reasonable. "Can I speak to Jackie?"

"She's at Marnie's."
Isabel hung up.

Jackie and Marnie were making strawberry daiquiris when Joanne called.

"The media is at your mother's house and she may call you. Your father and I think you should stay at Marnie's tonight, if that's okay with the Sikes'."

Joanne wanted to help Zach. She could tell Isabel's call was stressing him.

"Marnie, can I stay over tonight?" The two giggled. "Of course." Marnie said.

"What's going on at Mom's?" Jackie asked.

"We're not certain, only that photographers were at her door."

"Ok, thanks Joanne. Tell Dad I love him... and love you, too." Jackie hung up and hit the blender.

"So what's going on?" Marnie asked.

"I don't know. My mother is wigging out I guess and bugging Dad and Joanne."

"Did you tell Joanne my parents are out of town?"

"Hell no."

They both laughed and cranked up the Bose sound system. Their anthem started and they began to dance around, singing No Doubt's "Just a Girl" into wooden spoons and spatulas.

The phone rang again but the girls couldn't hear it over the music.

Isabel left a message on Marnie's home answering machine, "Jackie is to call her mother immediately!"

CHAPTER SIX

K en sat on his favorite barstool sipping a dirty martini. "Can we change the channel?"

"What channel?" The bartender pointed the remote at the small TV on the end of the bar.

"Entertainment Tonight."

Billy obliged and wiped the counter next to the small black and white set. Ken knew the older man liked to keep up with sports, namely the Rams, even though they had moved to St. Louis. Most often the TV couldn't be heard, unless Billy was monitoring a game.

"Just looking for some gossip, Billy." Ken was in a good mood.

Billy was his favorite bartender in West Hollywood; he adored the 63-year-old grandfather of seven who had been married to the same woman for 45 years. He was a good listener, an excellent bartender, and he knew the entire scope of Ken's romance with Evan—beginning to end.

Ken formed two friendships in LA when he got off the bus from Lubbock, Evan and Billy. He met Evan in a gay bar the first afternoon he rolled into LA and Billy later that night, after Evan had gone home. Ken was madly in love with Evan and he told Billy that night.

Billy listened and didn't judge. So Ken became a regular during Billy's shift at the MelRose bar. It was a small bar at the corner of Melrose and Poinsettia with a neon sign that blinked alternately in green and red "Mel" and "Rose".

Ken moved to LA via Greyhound. A documentary on the life of Martin Luther King, Jr. gave him the idea for his mode of transportation. Though he would *take* public transportation, as opposed to boycotting it, he thought it was symbolic that he take his own *freedom express* on April 4th, the anniversary of King's assassination.

He thought about his own minority status and it empowered him to get on a bus and go live where he blended in. He told his mother he wouldn't be back.

It wasn't like anyone would miss him. He was just the crazy queer kid who helped his mother in her salon after his dad had long given up bonding with him. He and his mother loved to read Silver Screen and they both had a crush on Rock Hudson.

His mother even encouraged him to be an actor in high school, but it didn't work out because he certainly wasn't going to kiss a girl. So he just did his best to be the class clown and laugh off his pain and confusion.

Billy pointed to the screen.

Ken's mouth flew open. Mark Collins was being interviewed by Mary Hart.

"I thought he was dead?" Billy said. "That was the rumor."

"Missing," Ken corrected him, reading the caption under Collins image on the screen. "Great, he's written a book."

Billy turned up the volume.

"No Mary, I've not been in touch with Joanne Manning," Collins sounded professional, less cocky. "This is my story. I'm not ashamed to call myself a tabloid journalist. It's what I do." Collins hoped to rattle the Mannings' cage by being on TV.

Hart countered, "If this is about you, why is the book titled *Joanne's Story?*"

"Because I broke her story. She made my career."

"Some believe you *broke her* and that's what made your career. But if that was your career defining moment, why have you been in hiding for 3 years?"

Ken mumbled to Billy, "I could kiss Mary right now."

"I've actually been writing a couple of books and it's taken this long. Hiding might be a fair enough assessment. I needed to clear my head and get to work." Collins wasn't going to fall for her tactics. He also knew if the Vasquez book was a hit, he could surely cash in on Joanne's.

"Clear your head?" Mary repeated, short of her mouth falling open.

"Well, Mary, you know the pressures we're under," Collins wanted viewers to realize she was cut from the same cloth as him.

"We are not employed by the same company, Mark. But I do want to thank you for taking time to…" Billy turned the TV down.

"I wonder if she'll see this," Ken was referring to Joanne.

"You still in touch?" Billy asked.

"Not really. I got her some connections for the PBS documentary, but Zach asked me to let her heal. Basically, back off." Ken pushed his empty martini glass toward Billy for a refill.

"What are you going to do?"

"Talk to my attorney, I might need a restraining order."

"From the tabloid guy?"

"No, Marquel," Ken replied.

"You mean Joanne," Billy corrected.

"No, Marquel. I don't know Joanne, really. But I do know Marquel."

CHAPTER SEVEN

Collins was pleased. He peered into his extended lens and watched. He recognized the motorcycles and vehicles of his old comrades. There was one set back from the rest, but perhaps this one wasn't part of the crew. It was a celebrity neighborhood, after all, and everyone had their routes.

From his perch atop a balcony in a rental house not far from Isabel Manning's home, he took some great shots of the second wave of paparazzi. It was easy to hire his old buddies on a slow night. He paid them well and he owned the shots.

Collins knew Isabel would be looking for the publication where they'd appear and it would drive her crazy. He had no intention of publishing her picture, except on his wall of shame. And if his photographer friends did sell her picture, he could care less.

The story of his book release and recent television interviews were breaking and things would soon fall into place. Or perhaps for some, things would soon fall apart.

The doctor's ex could get under anyone's skin and why not get her under Zach's and Joanne's? The method of *attack and observe* was used by a famed Hollywood cult to control members trying to escape. Practicing the technique on an unsuspecting Isabel Manning was the perfect welcome home, though he found it much too easy to mess with her head. It wasn't that he wanted Isabel's attention. He just wanted her to panic enough to stir up the couple.

"I don't know which is more fun... attacking, or observing," Collins muttered to himself.

It started with a dozen roses and a heated kiss when he got home.

Joanne had been writing her new seminar speech and was working at the computer in the breakfast nook. Zach began by unbuttoning her blouse as he read over her shoulder. She played along. She was glad Jackie was at Marnie's, she wouldn't want her walking in on them.

He spun her chair around and pulled her up to meet him in a kiss, then he moved on to her breasts and pushed the spaghetti strapped top off her shoulders, unzipping her skirt. He pulled the skirt down and her panties off in one swift move.

She had never met this Zach. His hands and mouth were moving all over her and she wasn't about to stop him.

He carried her to bedroom and worked feverishly to get inside her. She suspected that he had snorted cocaine, though she knew he had turned down Lou's offers before.

She didn't care. It was as if he had something to prove and she didn't want to stop him.

When they were both spent, Zach got up and made them scrambled eggs and pancakes. He seemed energized. He didn't dress. He was open, proud of his performance.

They made love again after the meal, but this time on the kitchen floor. Afterward Zach opened some champagne and they drank, played, tickled each other and made love again. She was getting drunk, but he still was wired.

They drank more and filled the tub with a bubble bath and got tangled in limber resolve.

"What are celebrating?" Joanne asked.

"Us," Zach replied.

He stood and picked up the slippery Joanne and carried her to the bed. He ran his hands over her breasts and stomach and poured some champagne into her navel. "I want to drink you in and die a happy man."

She laughed. "I'm going to be so hung over in the morning."

CHAPTER EIGHT

George was alone at a small table in the back of a dark honky-tonk, drowning his sorrows in beer and sad country and western songs. He drank a long pull from his malt liquor. Brooks and Dunn's "Neon Moon" began and Joanne started toward him.

He was focused on the bottle, but looked up when she approached. When the song came to the lyrics, "she'll come back someday…" he sang the words to her.

Joanne woke up.

For a split second she thought she was in bed with George and was relieved to see Zach. Her head was pounding from the champagne and she couldn't figure out why George was in her thoughts when Zach had given her the best sex of her life.

But nothing ever seemed to stop her nightmares. Or were they nightmares?

She remembered her grandmother telling her that if a departed loved one speaks to you in a dream, they were speaking from heaven.

Grandmother wanted Joanne to be reassured that she wouldn't be alone. She wanted to speak to Joanne in dreams. The older woman died of breast cancer when Joanne needed her most. She had barely known her parents. Each had passed at a young age from unexpected causes. Her father from a rattlesnake bite during a lone hunt and her mother from a fall off a ladder that caused brain swelling and a deteriorated vegetative state.

Joanne never dreamed about her grandmother or her parents speaking with her. But George was becoming a regular visitor... and now he was singing to her? She needed to share this with Dr. Wright. She wondered if he were in limbo or needed help moving on.

She didn't dream of Marquel and George together, and that bothered her. She wanted to know that George was caring for little Marquel. It was also becoming harder to see Marquel's face and hear her voice. She wondered if children could grow up in heaven. Would they even recognize each other? Now she wanted to cry.

She rolled over and watched Zach sleep. He looked wiped out in the morning light. She wondered if he would feel the same pounding headache that she did...

Then she remembered she hadn't started the letter to George that Dr. Wright recommended.

But what would she say?

CHAPTER NINE

Sophie Krentz munched on a baby carrot as she listened to her old college roommate, Isabel Manning, drone on about the media. They had been friends for years, though Isabel only really needed Sophie when the heat was on and she wanted to complain about Zach and Joanne.

Sophie loved gossip and was usually game to get the inside scoop, but today she was bored. She actually liked Joanne when she was the actress Marquel. She was a fresh face and ironically, that's where Isabel first met Joanne, at Sophie's party. At the time, neither Sophie nor Isabel had a clue that the woman was a patient of Zach's and that he was falling in love her. Such is Hollywood…

Isabel had liked Marquel, too. She was a rising star and everyone wanted to be a part of the A-list. But that changed quickly when Isabel learned the woman was a contender for her ex-husband's and their child's attention.

The shorter, rounder Sophie was trying to diet again and it was not going well. Isabel had arranged the lunch meeting and had no interest in listening to her friend, she wanted to be heard.

A waitress dropped off their drink order.

"Isabel, get to the point." Sophie sipped her tonic water.

"Don't be a bitch, Sophie." Isabel wanted her to care.

"No pictures were published in the trades," Sophie reminded her.

"Well, I'm hoping we can figure this out. The two of us."

Sophie shook her head. "We don't have to play sleuth."

Isabel's mouth dropped. "Where is the Sophie I know? The Sophie who used to love uncovering the hidden agenda?"

"Tired of guessing," the thick necked blonde replied. "Life's too short, Isabel. Speak while you can."

Isabel glared at her friend. It was hard enough to listen to Zach preaching at her, but Sophie!

"Don't give me the look, Isabel. Say it."

"Say what?"

"What's on your mind? Spit it out."

"Support me and be concerned, damn it!" Isabel snapped. "I don't need you talking down to me like Zach does."

A smile slowly spread across Sophie's face. "Now, isn't that better, Isabel?"

Isabel couldn't decide yet. "Thanks Soph."

"Did you catch *Entertainment Tonight*?" Sophie was trying to maintain her composure.

Isabel leaned in, "What?"

"I understand Mark Collins has a book signing on Saturday," Sophie gave her a wink.

Isabel beamed. "Wait... book signing?" Then realization hit, this wasn't just entertainment gossip.

"Uh huh."

"Mark Collins!" Isabel was loud.

"Shhh." Sophie said.

"Do you know what he wrote?" Isabel lowered her voice.

"It's called 'Joanne's Story', so..."

Isabel slapped the table hard. "I knew it..."

The restaurant went quiet.

A younger man dining near them knocked a water glass off his table and the crash of glass and ice caused Sophie to jump. He seemed intent on their conversation.

Isabel was furious, turning to face him down. "Mind your own damn business!"

"Could I have a few napkins from your table... to soak up the water," the man apologized to Sophie, but wouldn't make eye contact with Isabel.

"Knock yourself out," but before Sophie could offer him her napkin, he leaned in and grabbed Isabel's... which bore a perfect lipstick print.

Isabel watched, appalled, as he folded it neatly and put it in his jacket.

"Did you see that?" Isabel gaped at Sophie.

Sophie shook her head.

The man left, stepping over the glass and not bothering to look back. He left cash on the table.

"You're a bitch!" Isabel stood.

Sophie laughed. "You're getting all bent out of shape for what?"

"I knew this was about her! I told Zach, and you had the nerve to play coy."

"You're the center of attention," Sophie said matter-of-factly, glancing around.

The patrons were awaiting Isabel's next statement.

Isabel didn't notice. She was wondering where those photos of her would appear and under what context.

"You owe me." Isabel stormed off.

Sophie smirked.

The crowded restaurant went back to their conversations.

CHAPTER TEN

Zach put a slice of bread in the toaster. He decided to make a breakfast for both Jackie and Joanne. He was almost embarrassed to think about the lovemaking that had taken place in the kitchen a few nights before.

He and Joanne were so hung over the next day that they slept for 12 hours and stayed in, ordered in, avoided alcohol and just talked. A long, shared bath was followed by a gentler night of passion... and no television.

His anger with Lou was driving him in a way he hadn't anticipated. He felt like he was losing his mind. Out of control. He kept a small stash of cocaine in his golf bag that Lou gave him. He had never considered trying the drug, but he needed something that night, after Lou told him about Collins. The hate emotion aroused him in such an unexpected way. He wasn't certain how he would have reacted if Joanne rejected him.

He needed to tell her about Collins, Jackie too.

Jackie would be in college in a few months and soon it would be just him and Joanne. He would miss his little girl, but he liked the thought of being a couple. They hadn't much alone time after the wedding. Jackie moved in when Isabel left for Marseille during the first two years of his marriage to Joanne.

The toast popped up. One perfect and the other burnt. "That's it."

He pulled the plug from the wall and felt a jolt in his left hand.

"Damn, that hurts." He shook his hand, flexing his fingers. Then he grabbed the small appliance with both hands and thrust it in the trash. "Son of …"

Joanne walked in. "Are you okay?"

"No, the toaster ruined my surprise," he was becoming agitated. The thought of Collins and the electric shock were elevating his blood pressure again.

"I like burnt toast," Joanne laughed and kissed him lightly.

He wrapped his arms around her and another jolt seemed to reflex in his arm.

"Relax." She pulled back to look at him, to read his face. He seemed anxious. "Are you okay?"

"Lou called me…" Zach started.

"Did you hear?" Jackie entered the kitchen and poured herself a coffee.

"The noise?" Joanne queried. "Yes, your father just trashed the toaster."

"Huh?" Jackie was confused.

"I was trying to make breakfast…" Zach couldn't finish before Jackie interrupted.

"That reporter wrote a book about you, Joanne. It's called 'Joanne's Story'." Jackie stirred her coffee. "The entertainment shows have been buzzing about it for two whole days. I think the book jacket is a billboard somewhere around Studio City, I'm surprised you haven't heard."

"Mark Collins," Joanne took a step back from Zach.

"Yes," Jackie said. "That's his name."

CHAPTER ELEVEN

Dear George,

Dr. Wright said I should share my feelings with you.

I am very confused. I love Zach, and I have always loved you. I have never stopped loving you and I know we hurt each other, but we both have to let go.

I don't think you have, George. You continue to visit me in my dreams, but I don't see Marquel. Why can't I see her?

George, I don't understand what happened after I left. I'm sorry if I hurt you. I didn't think I could love you as you deserved. I hated myself so much. How could I love you?

Zach is the one person who knew me as the damaged mother who stole her daughter's name. I can't believe I did what I did. I have healed a lot.

I feel if you were alive, maybe we could talk. I'm not sure if we could be friends. I know how you are.

You close the door.

I guess that's how it really happened. You did close the door on me after I made an awful mistake. I couldn't get back into your heart after little Marquel died.

I never thought of it that way…

But why did you come after me after so long? Why did you come back to claim me when you saw what I was? Why did it matter then?

Was it just a familiar relationship? Was it just because I moved on?

But you learned the truth. I lost my mind.

I was no longer your Joanne. She died emotionally when Marquel died. That Joanne was a happy mother, married to her high school sweetheart. It was too hard for her to face you, George. To feel your pain and know she caused it. To miss her child and know she was at fault. It's too much to bear. She had to go somewhere emotionally and physically.

Please kiss Marquel for me. Hug her tight.

I can't write now. This is making me very sad.

Love you both,
Joanne

CHAPTER TWELVE

Joanne looked at her reflection in the dressing room mirror. "We're here to help others," she rehearsed.

She was distracted by thoughts of Isabel and Jackie. Lou Bartalow had called the house before they left for the studio and he apologized to her, but she didn't understand why he was apologizing. She wasn't certain what to make of the Collins news, except that Zach clearly wasn't himself.

She wondered when Zach knew and now she suspected their night of passion was somehow connected. Did he think he'd lose her again?

They didn't talk about it.

It was starting again. Their quiet denial. It was less painful than dredging up the past. They fell into a habit of avoiding subjects that would upset either one of them. As a medical professional he knew it wasn't healthy, and she couldn't do much to change the situation.

In some ways, both Zach and George had similar traits.

Both preferred to move on to another topic than address a painful conversation in which they played a part. The only difference was George was a fighter. He was willing to dish it out if he felt cornered and Zach would just not speak. Neither situation was healthy. George placed blame and didn't empathize, while Zach's silence sent her to her dark place, where she had inner dialogues and tried to find parts of herself that could cope.

Zach sat on the Green Room couch behind her reading the Wall Street Journal. He was used to her warm-up routine and it gave him time to unwind.

"Baby," Zach pulled his reading glasses off and addressed Joanne. He was sincere and looked tired.

Joanne looked at him in the mirror.

"I love you."

Joanne smiled at him. "I love you more."

"Not possible." He got up and began massaging her shoulders.

She turned to grab a quick kiss.

They seemed to find ways to be in the moment and cope, though never really addressing the tension between them. This felt especially hurtful to Joanne. It wasn't okay for him to avoid talking, when he pushed her to open up in sessions. When she did challenge him, knowing he'd counsel to the contrary, he just got quieter.

CHAPTER THIRTEEN

The line outside the bookstore was long.

"We need this stack signed before we open the doors. We'll hold them for a few VIPs and store display." The manager of the chain bookstore was going through the usual author event protocol.

Collins pulled the stack over and got the first one open when he heard a familiar voice behind him, "Your publicist asked if I wanted a copy and I said I'd pick it up personally."

Collins turned.

The store manager leaned in. "Ken Avery is on the VIP list."

Collins nodded to her and she moved about, straightening things.

Avery grabbed a book and pushed it in front of Collins. "Just make it—To Ken, the asshole who discovered Marquel."

Collins laughed. "Absolutely! You're right. Thank you." Collins wrote just what Ken requested in the book he was already holding open. He finished by signing his name large, covering the rest of the page.

Ken took the book. "I'd like to pummel you with this, but I suppose I should read it first. Have you talked with Joanne?"

"As I understand, she is no longer your client, so why do you care?" Collins went back to signing books from the stack.

The store manager reappeared, "We open in 5 minutes."

"I suppose you're right, Collins. This is between you and Joanne." Ken dropped the book to the floor and kicked it as hard as he could. The spine of the book snapped and a few pages flew loose.

"Missed your chance with the NFL." Collins then pointed to the approaching uniformed guard, "Mr. Avery was just leaving."

Ken wrestled his arm from the chunky guard. "Whatever the outcome of this piece of trash, I hope it finishes you."

Collins laughed, "I'm just getting started."

CHAPTER FOURTEEN

Dear George,

I am so glad you aren't alive to deal with what is happening. Our story is surfacing again in the media and it's so unfair that you can't be here to defend yourself. I have nothing but love for you, George, and I won't say anything that would stir your soul from resting.

I'm not really sure what our story is. Mark Collins wrote a book called "Joanne's Story" and I just feel robbed of the chance to say goodbye to you…

Zach and I haven't had an easy time, either. I love him and I know that hurt you. It wasn't intentional.

I'm still struggling with the choices I made. Maybe I shouldn't have come back to California. I have impacted Zach and Jackie's lives, which has made Zach's ex-wife lash out.

If I would have stayed with you in Florida, I'm not sure we would have been happy. You may have been comfortable having me there, but I think it would have eaten me alive to see Marquel's old room on a daily basis.

I guess… I get it now. Why you came for me. Our house was an empty place for you. You needed to fill it up and we could have tried to have another child. But I'm not capable of that. I'm not strong enough. I feel I'm a plague to the people I love.

I don't know if God is mad at me. Could you ask, George? Tell him I'm sorry I disappointed him.

Kiss little Marquel for me.

I miss her so.

CHAPTER FIFTEEN

Isabel was furious that she'd been under attack by photographers who were attempting to unnerve her at all hours.

She complained to the homeowners association and the security company she'd hired to protect her home. Zach didn't answer her calls. Jackie didn't answer her calls. Sophie wasn't supportive and Isabel was a nervous wreck.

When she stopped in the Sikes driveway, she was hoping the couple would be home, so she could talk with them about Marnie and Jackie's behavior. To her dismay, they were traveling again and let Marnie play house.

Isabel grabbed Jackie by the arm and pulled her from Marnie's front door.

Marnie watched from the window.

"If you ever ignore me again," Isabel screamed, "I will make certain you regret it. Hopping back and forth from Marnie's to your father's and not communicating. You are an impossible little bitch!"

Isabel was shaking.

"Don't you ever say that to me again, mother!" Jackie pulled from her grasp. "You're being overly dramatic, even Joanne wasn't this upset."

"Really! Is she under attack daily?" Isabel pulled her sunglasses off to make certain her daughter looked her into her bloodshot eyes. "You've not been home to see what Carmen and I are dealing with."

"How is Carmen?" Jackie asked.

"How is Carmen?" Isabel shook her head. "Really? You look me in the eye and ask… How is Carmen? Gosh, I guess you should ask *her* since you care so much."

Jackie rolled her eyes. She wasn't sure what her mother wanted her to do. "The reporter is trying to make money off Joanne's pain. He's a jerk."

"Her pain!" Isabel pushed the sunglasses back in place and crossed her arms.

"Grow up, mother.," Jackie said. "She lost her only child. You have no idea how that feels."

"I suppose I don't. But you are my only daughter and I'm feeling vulnerable." Isabel started to cry.

Jackie was shocked. Her mother rarely cried. She didn't like to see anyone upset.

Isabel was sobbing. "We've all suffered through her ordeal. Hell, how do we know what really happened to her husband?"

Jackie's mouth flew open. "Oh my God!"

"Hunting accident my ass!" Isabel snapped.

Jackie was stunned. She didn't know why her mother would focus on Joanne's ex. He died well after Joanne arrived in California.

CHAPTER SIXTEEN

Zach answered the landline. "Manning residence."

"I… hey, this is awkward." Ken mumbled.

"Who is this?"

"It's me. Ken."

"Oh, I forgot about you…" Zach's voice was tired.

"Thanks. I deserve that, but really, thanks for not hanging up."

Zach asked the only question that seemed relevant, "Have you read the book?"

Ken laughed. "I went to the signing in West Hollywood… and got thrown out."

"For punching the author, I hope?" Zach perked up.

"I'm too much of a pussy for that. But I did destroy the book by kicking it to hell and back. I was hauled out the front door to a long line of hungry fans. You'd think they'd want to escort me out the back, but no. Not in good 'ole Hollywood."

Zach's laugh was a welcome sound to Ken's ears.

"So how do we find out what's in the book," Zach inquired. "I'm sure as hell not buying a copy."

"Maybe ask Sophie Krentz?"

"Soph?" Zach seemed surprised.

"Miss scarfed-fatneck thought I didn't see her in line, but I did. And I am sure she was feasting on my moment."

"God, you made my day. I needed a laugh."

Ken was feeling better too. "So how is Marq… sorry, Joanne?"

"I'm not sure…" Zach sounded distant, "déjà vu."

It was creepy that they were again united in discussion for Joanne's well-being.

"I'm sorry I called." Ken lamented.

"I'm not. She may need you. Let's keep the lines of communication open." Zach's tone was encouraging.

"Now you made my day," Ken choked up a little.

CHAPTER SEVENTEEN

Dear George,

My heart is heavy. I have read the story Collins wrote about my life, well, our lives, and I'm convinced that I need to respond with the real story. I don't know if I am strong enough to write it.

His book is a bestseller. He's doing book tours and media interviews.

It makes me sick. I need to respond.

I promise to be honest and that means telling the truth about how I hurt you.

CHAPTER EIGHTEEN

Joanne waved as she walked across the seminar stage. The crowd of mostly women stood. The men in attendance were supportive husbands, boyfriends and a few gay couples. The applause continued until she asked them all to sit.

Her new speaking engagement was not approved by Dr. Wright. Her therapist wanted her to pace herself, as the media were following Joanne's every move now that the Collins book was such a success.

Joanne's pale pink Chanel suit hung loosely. She had lost another 10 pounds since Collins' book release. She couldn't maintain her appetite amid the stress, but her face still looked radiant on the monitors.

Dr. Wright and Zach were in the front row. They worried that the Q&A portion of her engagement could present challenges and were there to support her as best as they could.

Joanne, with wireless microphone, addressed her audience. "I am so pleased to see you all," she smiled and opened her arms to them.

The monitors on both sides of the stage picked up her sincere welcome. More applause.

"As you know, I am here to discuss overcoming obstacles… and… well we've all come to this place having overcome something."

The audience applauded themselves.

"I'm only going to take a brief moment to address this… I have to address the recent book that was written by tabloid journalist, Mark Collins." Joanne seemed to be in actress mode, drawing strength from the period during which she had worked on *Suburban Life*.

A few random shouts followed, such as "you tell it, sister" and then the packed hotel ballroom was silent again, the attendees glued to her every word.

"Mr. Collins is entitled to write whatever he pleases… but the truth will be written in the form of my own autobiography, I promise. If Joanne's story is to be told," she forced the words out with a lightness that she didn't quite feel, "who better to tell it than *Joanne*?"

The audience stood and applauded. Whistles and cheers continued for several minutes. She was touched by their love. She glanced down at Zach and put her right hand over her heart.

He responded to her silent declaration of love by blowing her a kiss. The monitors caught their moment and more cheers rose as the noise level reached its peak.

Mark Collins snuck into the back of the room in time to catch the gesture only, having missed his pseudo-introduction. He stood against the wall in shadow and mocked Joanne, putting his hand on his heart.

A female attendee turned and made visual contact with Collins. Thinking his mirroring of Joanne was sincere, she smiled at him and put her hand on her heart. He smiled back until she turned to the stage again, then rolled his eyes and dropped his hand.

Joanne maintained the composure of a politician on convention day, waiting until her guests were quiet again, and seated.

The moment was interrupted by a loud male voice, "Bitch! Reckless baby killer!"

Collins was startled by the outcry. *What the hell?* He couldn't tell at first where it was coming from.

Everyone turned, trying to see where the heckler was, and as quickly as the distraction drew attention to the rear of the auditorium, a loud POP-POP-POP sounded, followed by a thud at the stage.

Everyone was screaming in panic.

Joanne could hear their screams and see the rafters of the stage and the crisscross pattern of metal that housed the lighting. In her peripheral vision she saw the large TV screens and people mounting the stage, though all this was viewed sideways. Then Dr. Wright was touching her and other faces surrounded the doctor's. The faces closed in around her, tears streaking them and wide mouths crying and screaming.

"Can you hear me Joanne," Dr. Wright asked.

She couldn't speak, but her mind was calm.

Dr. Wright knelt close and spoke into her ear, "You're going to be all right. Focus on your breathing."

Joanne closed her eyes.

The blood coming from Joanne's abdomen was soaking her pink suit. It looked like a rose seeping out. Dr. Wright was being pushed and her elderly knees rubbed hard against the stage floor. She feared herself being wounded.

With all the strength she could muster and whole lot of anger the doctor stood and screamed, "GET BACK SO HELP ME GOD OR I WILL HURT YOU ALL!!!!"

The crowd was startled, and some of them even complied, but then hotel security pushed their way through and began pulling people off the stage.

Dr. Wright slowly got back down to her knees and spoke to Joanne.

"Joanne, you're going to the hospital and we'll…" she realized Zach wasn't there. "We'll be right beside you."

Then the doctor moved aside to let the event EMTs work.

Joanne blinked her eyes open and saw unfamiliar faces. She felt her body being handled, shifted. Her eyelids dropped and she returned to the shadows.

Zach was running after the gunman. Sirens could be heard amid the commotion.

Sheer adrenaline fueled him as he followed the male assailant. When he hit the metal bar to release the stage door, he felt sure he could take the man himself. He pushed through the enclosed hallway that was a passage for emergency exits and entourage getaways.

Zach was sure the gunman was Collins. He looked down the bare corridor and saw no one, but he could hear the clap, clap of shoes moving away from him.

But why would Collins run? Wouldn't he want credit for killing her?

Killing her. His mind just registered the thought.

He stopped in his tracks. Security guards and uniformed police rushed past Zach.

"We're going to get the bastard," one of the guards who recognized Zach from an earlier introduction that day reassured him as he sprinted past, gun drawn.

Zach took a deep breath and started after them. No sooner did he begin than he felt a stabbing pain in his chest. It was hard, crushing. It took his breath. He wanted to see Collins get caught, wanted to watch the beating—or whatever other torture—might ensue. He pushed his back to the cold concrete wall and placed a weak right hand in the middle of his chest, trying to catch his breath.

He wanted to avenge his wife's attacker, but now he regretted leaving her side.

He had already failed her in so many ways.

Why did he ask Lou to get Collins out of the country? Why had he run after the gunman and not to his wife's side? What emotions were driving him that would send him running away, and after... whom?

If he had just left the bastard to go about his business ruining their lives in the media… They could have moved on. They could have moved to a remote city or country. *FUCK!* His chest was crushing his air supply.

He was frozen to the spot, unable to move as his mind flashed all the pictures of their time together.

More people pushed through the door and past Zach, though it appeared to be curious onlookers and hotel staff. He went largely unnoticed aside from a passing nod here or there, though he hoped to gather enough breath to ask about Marq… *Joanne.*

What seemed an eternity of foot traffic and chattering was broken by a loud cry reentering the corridor.

"We got him!" Came a shout from the distance.

Zach nearly collapsed in relief. He hoped the gunman would be brought back inside where he could identify him as Collins, though he was only waiting now until he drew enough strength to return to the ballroom and find Joanne.

"They got him," he told himself, forcing air through his lungs. He took a step, then another…

Zach stumbled back through the auditorium door along with the curious and vigilante wannabes. The crowd had thinned. He still couldn't speak.

A few paramedics were still tending to those injured in the panic when an older woman waved one toward Zach. "I think he's having a heart attack," she pointed.

His ashen face was grimacing as he placed one finger on his nose in agreement. He took it as a good sign that Joanne was no longer there, which meant she was in an ambulance—or maybe a helicopter—but there was still hope she would survive.

The woman approached him gingerly. "Aren't you Joanne's husband?"

Zach nodded.

CHAPTER NINETEEN

Zach was strapped to a gurney and placed in an ambulance before he could even speak. He felt every twist and bump the vehicle made. The strap tightened on each sharp turn and he wondered if the oxygen he was receiving was being cut off.

He didn't really have the vision to focus on the EMT beside him, but whoever was there assured him Joanne was ahead of him in another ambulance.

Both were on their way to Cedars-Sinai. But he didn't trust the info. He knew they would guard from sharing too much with a patient in shock and he couldn't be sure Joanne was alive.

He wanted to believe, but now his heart was aching at the thought of losing her.

Zach's thoughts turned to Jackie. What would his baby girl be thinking? Where was she?

Then he thought of Isabel!

He didn't want his ex showing up at the hospital. "Could you…"

The ambulance attendant saw he was trying to speak. She looked at the blood pressure monitor and saw it spike.

"Relax, sir. Everything is fine. Your wife is already there."

Zach closed his eyes. He believed her.

Collins pulled into the emergency room parking lot and observed the LAPD-lined entrance.

A few ER physicians were triaging patients outside. Though the gunman was captured, they wanted to keep copycats away and divert curious fans from Joanne's arrival. Only the most serious conditions were admitted immediately.

A bank of reporters was taking up the sidewalk in front of the hospital.

Collins pulled out a pocket knife and tried to decide where to make his mark. He had never used the knife, but he wanted to get inside. It had dangled from his keychain for years and he wondered if it might be too dull. He closed his eyes and sliced into the pinky finger on his left hand, not feeling anything immediately.

"Jesus," he looked at the near severed digit. He felt lightheaded. He dropped the knife and forgot to shut his car door as he ran toward the ER.

An officer by triage saw Collins jogging in a stupor.

"My finger!" Collins shouted. He was feeling faint and stumbled against a black car. His blood smeared like wet paint on the dark surface.

The blue colored lights of a police-escorted ambulance distracted the officer momentarily. Everyone stopped triage and moved to bring the stretcher inside. Collins fell to the ground, catching himself with his left hand and screaming as gravel got in the wound.

"Help," he called.

Another ambulance pulled in and more commotion ensued. Collins wasn't sure he would be awake when someone discovered him. He yawned at the feeling that was drawing him to black out.

He sank into a squat on the pavement and began to cry. "Bitch! Oh my God." His second wind finally kicked in. "I need help! Joanne you dumb bitch! You fuck up everything!"

Collins tried to pick the gravel out and screamed again.

"Oh my God. I hope you live so I can kill you."

Then he heard a click next to this head.

A uniformed officer trained his revolver on the wailing Collins.

"Sir, I'm going to take you in for questioning."

Collins looked up in horror. "Can't you see I'm bleeding to death?"

The officer looked at the vehicle with the opened door and pushed a button on the radio he wore on his shoulder. "Suspect may drive a Volvo, license number..."

"I'm about to lose a finger here. What the fuck am I a suspect of?" Collins whipped around and saw his pocket knife on the ground next to his car. "That's where I was attacked!"

Ken picked up his phone.

"Hi Hon," Evan's voice was quiet.

"Ev, everything ok?" His heart felt the twinge it always did when he was surprised by Evan. Ken registered the term "Hon" as a positive, regardless of his reason for calling.

"Have you heard the news?"

Ken was wondering where Evan was at this moment. "What news?"

"Joanne."

"Oh that," Ken was disheartened that Evan was only calling to gossip about the Collins book.

"How can you say it like that?"

"Ev, it's just a stupid book," Ken was annoyed.

"Then you haven't seen the news." Evan paused to choose his words before continuing, "Ken, honey. Joanne was shot today."

"Oh my God! Oh my God! Is she alright? Where? When?"

"I'll pick you up." Evan spoke calmly. "We should be there. She may need you."

Ken's mind was racing; someone else had said that to him recently... But who? He couldn't think, he was shaking. "I can't breathe. Oh my God! Oh my God!"

CHAPTER TWENTY

Joanne saw George in a brilliant light.

He was coming toward her. Little Marquel was following behind him, giggling.

"Mommy!" The bouncy, blonde child carried wildflowers in her chubby hands.

Joanne ran to them and they all embraced.

"We're all together," Joanne marveled at the peace she felt.

"It's our time, Jo." George kissed her on top of her head and picked up Marquel. He bounced the child on his hip.

Joanne reached for Marquel. She wanted to hold her baby.

"Clear!" The doctors placed the paddles on Joanne's chest and in a jolt George and Marquel disappeared.

"No!" Joanne screamed inside. No one heard.

She was now in darkness, the light gone. Her heart was beating faster and her lungs taking in more breath.

"*I want to go back,*" she talked within the dimension that seemed devoid of time. She could hear what was happening around her physical body, but she was blinded.

She wondered if she was truly blind... if she was alive or in limbo. She wanted to go back to the light.

"Good girl," the voice seemed pleased with Joanne. "You'll be good as new in no time."

Another voice chimed in, "How is her husband doing?"

Joanne wondered how they knew she had just seen George? *Why didn't they mention Marquel?*

"Heart attack?" the doctor queried. "Undetermined as yet."

Joanne's mind was racing. *George? He looked fine. But how?*

"Her blood pressure has improved," the nurse spoke again.

"We'll proceed with surgery once she stabilizes."

Suddenly, Joanne saw Zach's face coming into focus.

Dear God… Where was she?

CHAPTER TWENTY-ONE

Zach opened his eyes to a sobbing Jackie.
He was rigged up to what seemed like dozens of monitors and machines and felt weaker than he'd ever felt before in his life.

"Don't die, daddy," Jackie had repeated the words more than once.

Zach wasn't sure what day it was, or what time of day.

"I'm so glad you're here, baby." His voice was just above a whisper.

"Mommy dropped me off," Jackie stood and wrapped her arms around him, careful not to dislodge any tubes or wires. "She wanted to see you, but she didn't know if they would allow an ex into ICU."

He wanted to return the embrace, but a smile was the best he could manage. "I'll remember that."

Jackie laughed, returning to the chair beside the bed.

"Joanne is still in surgery. There are guards posted everywhere and I'm not sure why? They caught the gunman," Jackie was somber.

"Would you do me a favor, baby?"

Jackie nodded. "Anything."

"I want you to stay with me tonight," Zach felt depressed. "I'm feeling blue, but it would make your old man happy to have a familiar face around."

Jackie was overwhelmed by his request. She didn't want to go home to an empty house and she was worried reporters might be stalking the property anyway.

"Sure daddy," she was relieved. "Tell you what, I'm starved. I'll go to the cafeteria and bring back a sandwich and just sleep in the chair."

He smiled again. "Let your mother know. Tell her I appreciate her concern."

"That will make her happy. I'll be right back, just rest," Jackie kissed his forehead.

Zach closed his eyes and listened to the noise of the medical equipment.

Jackie stopped by the nurses station on her way to the cafeteria.

A handsome young man in his mid to late twenties was behind the desk and Jackie almost blushed. "Excuse me, doctor..."

"I'm not the doctor," the muscular, tanned man in green scrubs laughed. He had brown eyes like hers and closely trimmed brown hair. She suspected his hair would be unruly if it weren't for the close cut. "I'm a nurse."

Jackie smiled. "Oh... I would like to know how my father is doing."

"Manning, 208?" He pulled the chart and glanced at a few things, weighing what he could share. "Massive heart attack, but stabilized. Looks like he has some blockage and the cardiologist will determine the course of action in the morning. Tonight we'll be watching him closely."

Jackie bit her lower lip. "Will he be okay?"

"I'm Josh, by the way," he held out his hand to shake hers. "Test results are still coming in, but may I ask... are *you* okay?"

Jackie felt hot tears sting her eyes as she let go of his warm hand. She had just enough time to throw on jeans and a t-shirt when her mother had picked her up. She must look awful!

"I'm not sure," she half-laughed as more tears welled in her eyes.

"He's stable right now and your mother is stable, too." Josh said.

Jackie realized he probably knew nothing about her family. "Joanne isn't … I mean… I'm not her daughter."

Josh grimaced. "I'm sorry, I heard husband and wife and just assumed."

Jackie took a deep breath, "No, it's okay. I guess you don't keep up with the trades."

"Trades?"

"Joanne Manning, my father's wife. She was an actress on Suburban Life a few years back."

"Oh, the Hollywood trades. No. I'm a science geek, I barely watch movies," he seemed embarrassed.

"Suburban Life was a TV series," Jackie corrected.

"I'm guessing your family is famous and I'm like the only person who doesn't know who they are."

"I'm glad you're clueless," her relief was sincere. "I don't want to answer a million dumb questions right now."

"Dumb questions… clueless. You know me so well," he laughed.

Jackie realized what she'd just said. "I meant… a million questions."

"Dumb question number one: what is your name, famous girl?"

"Jackie Manning. Please don't feel bad about not knowing Hollywood drama. I only wish I could forget." Jackie's stomach growled audibly.

Josh laughed. "I think Jackie Manning's hungry."

"Good diagnosis, doc… I mean, Nurse Josh. That sounds weird."

"Just Josh will do."

"Could you point me in the direction of the cafeteria?" Jackie held her stomach.

"Just take the south elevator to the street level and you'll see the signs," he maintained eye contact with her until she looked away.

Jackie felt a blush rise to her cheeks. She didn't remember a word he said now.

"Ok," she just moved in the direction he pointed. "Thanks."

It was going to be a long night, but she was sort of hoping Josh would be there.

CHAPTER TWENTY-TWO

Evan and Ken arrived at the hospital hours after their intended departure from Ken's place. Ken had collapsed into Evan's arms upon seeing his former lover.

Local news affiliates had them up-to-date on the shooting of Joanne Manning, and her husband Zach's believed heart attack.

The media named their story the JoZac Attack and the brief footage from Joanne's speech was running non-stop with medical experts and ballistics weighing in. Old *Suburban Life* clips were also airing as the Marquel story was recapped.

"How could one family survive so much tragedy," the talking heads were repeating over and over. They were thrilled with how much mileage they could get from an actress who lost her child years earlier, only to lose her mind through a fugue state, rise to stardom and fall… and then reinvent herself under her true identity, help others, and be savagely shot in front of her fans! Brilliant!

Will she live?

Will her husband live?

Who is the gunman? They hadn't even gotten his story yet.

Some networks already had charts and timelines on all of Joanne's major life events. Zach was barely a blip on the radar, but they would build his story in the hours to come.

And where was Mark Collins, whose book *Joanne's Story* was still on the bestseller list? All the affiliates were bidding on getting his exclusive.

Ken and Evan stayed glued to the TV for far too long and one thing led to another—reassuring touches turned to tangled sheets and a heated hour of make-up sex.

As Jackie exited the cafeteria with her tuna sandwich and chocolate milk, she ran into Ken and Evan in the hallway.

"Oh my God," Ken hugged her spontaneously. He didn't care if he hadn't had any real relationship with the girl prior. They were family now, somehow.

Jackie didn't resist Ken. She was happy someone cared.

"I'm on my way up to see daddy. Joanne is out of surgery, but no one is allowed to see her. Guards are posted outside her door. I'm worried about her."

"Doll, we'll find out. Have you and Evan met?" Ken pointed to his lover.

"Nice to meet you. You let Marquel–" Jackie stammered, "I mean Joanne, live with you both when she first came to Hollywood, right?

Evan nodded, digging his large hands into his loose khaki trousers and letting Ken lead the discussion.

Evan was the epitome of the strong silent type. A towering, aging surfer with movie star features, he was charming and rugged with a soft laugh that made his perfect smile brighten a conversation. Most people couldn't imagine what such an intelligent businessman would see in a needy, high maintenance lover like Ken.

Evan was also chief financial partner in Ken's agency, and a wise investor. He worked little, soaked up the sun and had just doted on Ken during their time together. Since they broke up Evan spent more time trading stocks and less time in the sun. As he amassed more wealth, he began to lose his toned physique.

"Follow me," Jackie directed them.

Once they arrived in the intensive care wing, they could tell something was wrong. No one attended the nurses station.

Jackie bolted for Zach's room. The curtain was shut and people were talking as she pulled the curtain back. At first all she saw were the backs of hospital personnel, the monitors were making a lot of noise. Ken and Evan maintained a discreet distance just outside the doorway.

Jackie caught a glimpse of her father as the staff moved around him. He looked limp.

"Daddy!" she cried out.

Josh looked up, startled by Jackie's presence. He turned to her, walking her toward the doorway. "We're doing everything we can, Jackie."

Josh locked eyes with Evan, pleading silently for him to take Jackie outside. Evan escorted both Ken and Jackie into the hallway, uncertain what they were witnessing.

"Let's find a waiting room. The doctors need to do their job," Evan walked like he knew where he was going, looking for someplace they could sit Jackie down.

Jackie was shaken and followed Evan's lead without knowing why.

Ken put an arm around her shoulder, pulling her close. "We're here for you, don't you worry."

Joanne dreamed she was standing on the shore of the California coast. She was bathed in a warm light that drew her to the foaming Pacific waves that rushed up to the shoreline.

She was at peace with herself here. This was the place where reality existed.

She could smell the salt air and feel the soft sand sinking beneath her steps. The setting sun drenched her in a warm embrace.

It didn't matter what else was happening in the world, time was irrelevant. Serenity was hers. She could stay in this place and let God and nature heal her.

CHAPTER TWENTY-THREE

Collins was now in police custody with his newly stitched left pinky and several bruises from the handling he received by LAPD.

He had already called his lawyer and refused to talk, though the detectives persisted in extracting what they could from him.

Collins knew the drill. He had been a police reporter during a brief stint for local papers before coming to LA. He wasn't going to say shit.

If he could survive the cartel and make it back to states, he was stronger than these candy-asses. Whatever brutality they wanted to inflict was a walk in the park compared to what he'd seen in Bogotá.

CHAPTER TWENTY-FOUR

Ken paced the waiting room and shooed people out who wanted to turn on the television set. He convinced Jackie to eat while Evan set out to find out what was happening.

Evan was his rock; whatever needed to be done, Evan would surely do it calmly and only filter what Ken could handle.

"Doll, I'm wondering who can speak for Joanne?" Ken was more talking to himself and letting Jackie listen.

"I heard her attorney is handling everything, since daddy is her only family and not able to help." Jackie slurped her milk to the bottom of the carton.

"Is she still with Rosenberg?"

"I'm not sure. Oh, but I think they're consulting with Dr. Wright, too." Jackie was surprised she even recalled as much. "Dr. Wright and daddy were at the seminar when…"

Ken and Jackie both welled up.

Evan returned, quiet.

Ken and Jackie were both were taken aback by Evan's drawn expression. "I wish there was an easy way to say this, Jackie," he hesitated.

Ken closed his eyes and held his mouth. He feared what was coming next.

"Your father passed," Evan spoke firmly. He wanted her to hear it as fact.

"No!" Jackie screamed.

"I'm so sorry," was all Ken could get out.

"You two kept me from him! I could have said goodbye," Jackie slapped Ken in a rapid succession of hard hits as Ken began to weep and double over. He was horrified and shocked at Jackie's reaction.

Evan grabbed Jackie and hugged her close. He let her wail and break down, but he desperately wanted to hold Ken. He hadn't seen Ken so lost and hurt.

"You can still say goodbye," Evan encouraged. "Your father is still in his room."

"I don't want to see my daddy dead." Jackie pulled away from Evan and sank to the floor. "Oh my God, I hate everyone."

Evan sat down next to Ken and held him.

Ken was quiet and shaking. He put his head on Evan's shoulder and sobbed.

Josh walked in and nodded to Ken and Evan, then sat on the floor next to Jackie.

"Your dad gave me a message for you," his was the only calm presence in the room.

Jackie's face contorted with each painful sob. She tried to listen, but kept shaking her head, no.

"When you can focus," Josh said. "Try to breathe deeply."

He demonstrated a few deep breaths and slowly, she began to follow suit.

"What did… he say," Jackie started to sob again.

Josh encouraged her to resume deep breathing, and waited until her breaths were slow and calm before he spoke again.

"He said, tell punkin not to worry. I love her and I'll always be there for her," Josh's voice broke as he teared up, but maintained his composure.

Jackie was silent for a long time, but she kept breathing deeply.

"I want to see him," she said finally. Then she looked up at Ken and Evan. "I'm sorry..."

The men nodded their understanding.

"Don't be," Ken's voice cracked.

"I want to see him now," Jackie decided.

CHAPTER TWENTY-FIVE

The gunman's story began airing with regular frequency in the following days.

Adrian Dane Jackson, 25, a clerk at a local men's retail outlet was purported to have purchased a copy of *Joanne's Story* at an LA book signing. While in line at the signing, he witnessed the expulsion of a protester and upon reading the book became enraged.

Jackson's neighbor shared with the local ABC affiliate that he lived near the chain bookstore and frequented signings with Jackson. Jackson was a collector of memorabilia. He began by collecting autographs and moved on to oddities associated with famous people when he moved to LA from Oklahoma at 21.

Jackson also liked to pick through trash outside of celebrity homes. A used Kleenex, toothpick or wad of paper was gold to the Okie. Jackson's neighbor said that Jackson told him someday he would sell all his memorabilia and retire with a million dollars in the bank.

Ken had been reading to Evan from the paper, "...saw an argument in the bookstore, a man kicking and throwing copies of *Joanne's Story* shortly before the public was let in."

Evan took the paper from Ken. "We're not reading this garbage. You aren't responsible for what this Jackson guy did."

"Yes, I am. That asshole thought I was protesting Joanne." Ken grabbed the paper back from Evan, but not before it tore.

"You need to get dressed. The wake starts in two hours and you have to help Jackie keep it together." Evan was firm.

Ken tossed back a shot of scotch. "Oh my God, what about Joanne," Ken poured another. "… Keeping her in an induced coma at Dr. Wright's orders. What the fu…"

Evan took the bottle and the remains of the newspaper and began tidying up the space around Ken, "We're not the medical professionals. Get dressed."

Evan was already in his suit trousers, white ribbed tank and wing-tipped Florsheims. He wore underwear on special occasions. He preferred loose clothing and freedom of movement, but packed his goods in new white briefs for weddings, funerals, bar mitzvahs, first communions and graduations.

"God Ev, you just don't get it!" Ken threw his shot glass against the wall. "Joanne doesn't even know he's dead! This is so fucked up!"

Evan left the room.

"Where are you going?"

Evan returned with a broom and dustpan. "I know! We just went through that with Jackie!" His voice was raised this time.

It sobered Ken somewhat. He knew Evan.

The night wouldn't end well if Ken didn't calm down. Evan had tons of patience and once he snapped it got ugly. When Evan finally reached his limit he'd give Ken a detailed list of every moment he tolerated from their relationship, followed by a departure and no communication for days, weeks or months depending on the severity of the argument.

"Ev, honey. I'm sorry." Ken tried to help his lover but ending up getting a shard of glass in his toe. "Ah, I'm bleeding."

"Get in the shower and get a bandage on. I'm not leaving. But so help me God, I'm considering it." Evan grabbed a tissue and pulled the glass out of Ken's toe, dabbing the hardwood floor where the blood had dripped. He wrapped another tissue over the wound and Ken hopped out of the room.

Ken tried to change the subject, turning on the shower.

"What should we do for Jackie?" He shouted over the running water.

Evan ignored him. He knew Ken's defensive mode.

"Maybe a stuffed animal…" Ken began to cry. "Oh God… oh God… I don't know what to do."

CHAPTER TWENTY-SIX

Joanne struggled in the darkness. She could hear people at times and feel her body being moved, poked, elevated, and when she was feeling very hot, cool water bathed her. There was no way to tell them how she felt. How much she wanted to open her eyes and see where she was.

She tried to understand what brought her to this place. She was blind to sight as she formerly knew it, but saw so much more. Or was she remembering? It seemed everyone she loved was popping in to greet her.

At times she wasn't sure of her age. She saw her parents and the place she lived as a small girl. Then little Marquel appeared and she'd wonder how could they both be children. What was this place where time seemed obsolete?

She marveled at how Marquel was playing with the grandparents she had never met in real life. What was real?

Joanne remembered acting and dressing as a child for the telethon and reading the *Velveteen Rabbit*. It was a story that focused on what was real. The unreal became real, as it seemed to happen here.

Zach danced with her like he did at their wedding.

"I love you so much." Zach kissed her neck and whispered in her ear, "I want you to take care of Jackie, promise."

"Of course, we'll both care for her," Joanne laughed.

Dr. Wright sat by Joanne's hospital bed reading. The recliner was taller that she, as it was her legs barely touched the floor.

She heard Joanne audibly say, "Of course." Then she watched as Joanne rocked her head from side to side, smiling.

The doctor removed her glasses and looked at the IV drip. She wondered what Joanne was experiencing. She could only hope that when her patient was healed from the gunshot wounds and surgeries, she would see that happy smile again.

CHAPTER TWENTY-SEVEN

Isabel and Lyle were in the front row of the funeral home when Jackie came in from the back. They had the room to themselves for a half-hour before the public viewing would begin.

Jackie was somber and in denial.

Zach was in repose in an open casket lined in draped white satin.

He looked good, like he was only sleeping. Jackie walked in and kissed him on the forehead. Isabel began to sob and called for Jackie to sit next to her.

Jackie turned to her mother, one hand resting on her father's shoulder. "Daddy's ok," Jackie told Isabel. "He explained a lot to me when Marquel's identity was revealed."

"Don't Jackie," Isabel couldn't contain herself.

"No mommy, daddy loved her. He understood the loss she suffered and he told me that when someone passes, it's the people left behind who suffer. The people who die have no pain. He said we'll all be together again someday." Jackie was calm, though tears ran off her cheeks.

"You are so much stronger than I am." Isabel dabbed her makeup carefully with Lyle's handkerchief. "He was the better parent."

Silence followed, until Isabel nodded toward Zach and laughed. "Well, I'm sure he's enjoying the fact no one's disagreeing with me right now..."

Then Jackie started to laugh, and Lyle, too.

A photographer entered from a side door and Jackie nodded for him to come in.

"You're sure you want to do this?" Isabel asked Jackie. "Do we know we can trust him?"

"She's always suspicious," Jackie said to the cameraman. "She's worried you'll share these with the press."

"Oh, no I wouldn't," the short bald man in the navy suit approached Isabel. "My business is funeral photography. That's all I do."

He handed her a business card, letting his camera rest on the red tie on his belly. The strap about his neck wasn't long, nor was the photographer. His body was round at the stomach while everything else seemed lean and in proportion.

"The negatives are archived in a safe. I only shoot the deceased. There are many families who need the photos as a way to remember their loved ones through all stages of life, which includes the final farewell."

Isabel turned to Jackie. "How did you find this man?"

"My name is Charles Worthington," he interjected.

"I asked the funeral director, mommy." Jackie made the formal introductions. "Charles, this is my mother, Isabel Manning, and this is Lyle Herlbert."

The two men shook hands.

Then Jackie turned to the coffin and said, "This is my father, Zachary Manning."

"Very dignified," Charles nodded. "Do you want to be in any photos?"

"I only want them for Joanne. Please include a photo of his hands, too. Though I suppose I wouldn't mind a photo of me standing next to daddy. For myself. But the others I will give to Marq... I mean Joanne."

Isabel perked up. "I think I would like to be in one next to Jackie. A supportive shot."

Jackie turned to her mother, concerned. "Mother, these photos aren't for others to see. You have to promise me."

Charles began checking angles and focusing his lens as the women spoke.

"You can delay the delivery of the photos," he offered Jackie, but continued working.

Isabel drew closer to Jackie and Charles began directing them.

"First, let's have just Jackie in a side view. If you would, place your hand on the side of casket and look at your father." He took a number of rapid-fire shots. "Good. Now Isabel, please stand next to Jackie and perhaps put your hand on her waist or shoulder, whatever feels natural."

Isabel moved to the head of casket and placed her hand on Jackie's, her face was in view and only the side of Jackie showed. Charles took several shots and then repositioned Isabel at Jackie's side and a took a few more.

"Thank you," Charles said.

"May I have a set of the photos," Isabel asked. "After all, he is my daughter's father."

"He wouldn't want that, mother," Jackie said. "This is for Joanne, since she can't be here."

Charles looked at his watch. "Your guests will be arriving soon. I will contact you when the photos are ready, Jackie. I understand your wishes. It was nice to meet you," he nodded and left the mother and daughter to work things out.

Isabel followed behind him. "I expect to receive the ones I'm in."

"I was hired by Jackie Manning and she'll distribute any photos as she desires." Charles turned to Jackie, "I'm sorry for your loss, dear. You are a lovely young woman. I'm sure your father is happy you are attending to his final wishes."

Jackie walked over and hugged Charles. "Do you really think so?"

"I know so." Charles reciprocated the hug.

The wake lasted two hours longer than scheduled.

Zach's professional colleagues and Joanne's charity contacts continued to pay their respects in a steady succession. Jackie held up well and it was Ken and Evan's support that gave her the most comfort, aside from her mother.

Lou Bartalow apologized to Jackie, though she couldn't understand his reasoning. She figured his grief was making him confused. Marnie Sikes and her parents were early to arrive and late to leave.

Marnie shocked Jackie. She figured her best friend would be calm, maybe even bored at the wake, but instead Marnie was one of the most emotional people to attend.

"I don't know how you and Joanne are going to deal with this. I miss your dad already and he's not even my dad," Marnie hiccuped sobs in between rubbing her nose with a tissue. She looked like someone with a very bad cold or allergy. The whites of her eyes were red and her nose was chafed from all the rubbing.

Isabel motioned to the funeral director to bring in more tissues and to call it a night. Then she addressed Ken and Evan, "I appreciate your being with Jackie at the hospital. I realize we don't really know each other, but I'm sure in time that might change. Given the estate..."

Ken looked at Evan, wondering if his lover knew what she was talking about.

"We don't follow," Evan replied.

"Well, Jackie and Joanne are the only survivors to his estate and I'm just assuming you might be managing Joanne's affairs," Isabel addressed Ken.

"Oh," Ken didn't want to say anything further. His contract with Marquel was no longer in effect. He had never had a contract with her as Joanne Manning. He also found the whole matter rather ugly to talk about in front of Jackie.

As the last people departed, Jackie, Isabel and Lyle discussed the funeral service that would begin at 11 am the next day. They knew more flowers would arrive in the morning and they weren't certain if they should take them all to the graveside.

A persistent knock drew their attention. Jackie stepped into the funeral home lobby and saw a man in jeans, a navy blazer, white t-shirt and loafers. She wondered if he was lost or maybe worked at the place and got locked out.

The funeral director opened the door. "We are closed for the evening, sir."

"Jackie," the man called out. "I'm sorry I'm late."

Josh pushed a handful of wildflowers through the opening.

"Josh?" Jackie approached. "You didn't have to…"

"Yes, I had to."

The funeral director stepped aside and let him enter, and Josh immediately hugged Jackie.

She breathed in the scent of spice and pine in his cologne. "We were just about to leave."

"I have to work in the morning. I can't make the funeral but I would like to pay my respects."

"Sure." Jackie took the flowers he offered, loosely wrapped in green tissue paper.

"Those are for you," he said. "I know your father has plenty."

She found him funny. "You certainly have a way with words."

"Well once you get to know me, you'll see it never ends." He offered her his hand. "I know you need to go home, but would you take me in? I promise I won't be long."

She took his hand and led him in to the viewing.

Isabel and Lyle were surprised by the handsome man, noticeably older that Jackie.

"Mother, Lyle, this is Josh," Jackie introduced them. "He was one of daddy's nurses."

"A pleasure," Josh said. "I see Jackie has the best of both of her parents."

Isabel blushed. Jackie was a little surprised by her mother.

"Josh wanted to pay his respects, he can't make the funeral tomorrow."

"Very thoughtful of you," Lyle said and shook his hand.

"I know you need to get home, so if you don't mind."

They stepped aside and Josh jogged up to the open casket.

He talked openly, "You look great, Zach. Man, I wish this had turned out differently."

Josh placed a hand on Zach's shoulder, his nose began to run. "You fought the good fight, you know. I'm a man of my word," he choked on a sob. "You rest now."

Jackie brought a box of tissues to him.

"I'm one of those. An emotional sap." He wiped his eyes and nose.

Jackie teared up. His emotion touched her, "Me, too."

"I'd hate to see us watch a sad movie," he laughed.

Isabel and Lyle stood quiet. Isabel wondered if the man knew he was flirting with a seventeen-year-old.

CHAPTER TWENTY-EIGHT

Collins was cited for stalking once eyewitnesses placed him at both the scene of the shooting and at the hospital. It was evident from the book's release that Collins had a prior history following Joanne Manning when she was known as Marquel, but he was released and cleared of any wrongdoing surrounding the JoZac Attack.

Collins wanted to know what had driven Adrian Jackson to shoot Joanne.

The gunman's actions had foiled his attempt to harass the couple, and Zach being dead took a lot of the fun out his plans.

Jackson met Collins at the glass window of the maximum security visitor's booth. They both picked up their receivers.

"I don't know you," Jackson hung up the phone and stood.

"Wait," Collins flailed his arms. The younger man in the orange jumpsuit flipped him the bird and walked away.

Collins didn't give up. He came back every visiting day for two weeks until the shooter finally agreed to talk.

"My lawyer says I shouldn't talk to you," Jackson was quiet.

He sported a black eye this time and lacked the spirit he did on their first meeting. Collins figured some of the inmates must've ganged up on him, his linebacker build indicated a guy who could probably take care of himself otherwise.

"How are you holding up?" Collins feigned concern.

"Peaches, asshole." Jackson spit at the glass. "Now what the fuck do you want?"

"To tell your story," Collins shrugged.

"Let me ask you something. I read your book... and I read between the lines. You see that bitch for who she really is. A baby killer, right?" Jackson had a wild look in his eyes as he read the reporter's face carefully.

Collins wasn't certain how to respond, so he didn't.

"I thought so," Jackson calmed down. "My story isn't the same kind of story as Joanne's. Her story is full of her Hollywood lies, but you exposed the little bitch for who she really is. So I took care of her. My story is truth, and conviction."

Collins noticed Jackson's eyes were cocked a little to left, like he was staring into another dimension. He wasn't speaking to Collins at all. He was talking to himself. Collins wondered where Jackson's collector personality fit in?

"Buddy," Collins tried to snap him out of the fixation. "Do you know where Joanne is?"

"Heard she was in the hospital dying," Jackson laughed. "Maybe now she's got a taste of her own medicine."

Collins thought he might have a point. "What if she doesn't die?"

Jackson grinned, "I'm here, you're there. Nothin' stopping you."

Collins laughed. He was genuinely entertained by the man's insanity.

Jackson pleaded guilty before the judge. His defense attorney was speechless. He hadn't a chance to say the first word when Jackson blurted out his guilt from the defense table.

"I killed the baby killer!" Jackson's pride was evident, though he didn't seem to understand that his victim was indeed alive.

Jackson then proceeded to beat his head on the table. It took three police officers to control him and carry him out. He was tranquilized, declared insane shortly thereafter and moved to a state institution.

His collection of celebrity memorabilia sold for a few hundred dollars and, strangely, his own belongings became more collectible to dealers in the macabre.

CHAPTER TWENTY-NINE

"Will she be able to walk?" Jackie asked Dr. Wright. The two women stood by Joanne's bedside.

"In time… she'll need extensive rehabilitation, but she has healed nicely from her physical wounds. I'm concerned how she will process Zach's passing," the doctor spoke softly.

"Is she going to wake up soon?" Jackie wondered how long it would take to bring Joanne out of the medically induced coma.

"It's a gradual process. I've asked Ken and Evan to visit, too. She needs familiar faces greeting her daily." Dr. Wright assured the teen, "And I'll be here. Of course."

"But how does it work?"

"Each person is different. The drugs have kept her brain resting while she healed," Dr. Wright didn't want Jackie to think it was like turning a switch. "She may not even try to speak immediately."

Jackie turned her attention to Joanne's resting figure.

The doctor continued, "Her past trauma may cause resistance, coming back may take a period of adjustment. She may get frustrated. We just won't know."

"I brought my homework," Jackie put her backpack on the chair next to Joanne's hospital bed. "I'll try to be here as often as I can."

"Yes, I heard you graduate soon. Congratulations," Dr. Wright perked up. "Have you chosen a college?"

"UCLA. I'm not certain what I want to major in. But I'll get my general ed out of the way," Jackie began unloading her bag.

"You'll figure it, out. Are you going to live on campus?"

Jackie nodded. "I can't stay at daddy's. It's too depressing, and mommy's is stressful. She is obsessed with daddy's estate."

"Oh." Dr. Wright didn't want to probe. She stroked Joanne's hair instead, wondering what the coming days would bring.

CHAPTER THIRTY

Jackie couldn't concentrate. She kept thinking she'd seen Joanne moving her lips, and even stretch a finger once, but she couldn't be sure.

Though she'd spent a dreadful night at the same hospital when her father died, Jackie didn't have the fear or loathing of the hospital she had anticipated. She was there to help. She wanted her daddy to rest peacefully, and Joanne to know that she wasn't alone.

Jackie thought about Joanne's daughter, Marquel. She wondered how old the little girl would be today.

The child was three... or maybe four... when she died. Joanne went missing and wasn't discovered by George for almost a year and a half. Then Joanne went back to Florida with George and later married Zach and that was three years... Jackie guessed Marquel would be eight or nine by now.

She opened her biology book and tried to study. This was not a subject she cared about. She reread several paragraphs, trying to focus on the assignment, but it was not sinking in.

"I guess I'm going to read my biology text to you, Joanne." Jackie moved her chair closer to the bed. "This is not a course I would choose, but it's required, so here goes. Maybe we'll both learn something."

A knock came at the open door.

Jackie looked up to see Josh standing there. "Oh, I could use you right about now."

"I bet you say that to all the guys," Josh smiled.

She shook her head, indicating his joke had fallen flat. "I was going to share this lovely biology chapter with Joanne. I figured we'd make some flash cards and quiz each other."

"Don't let me stop you," he said.

"I wasn't going to," Jackie quipped, suppressing a smile.

"I would be happy to study with you later. Say 6 p.m.? There's a diner nearby on San Vicente Blvd., we could grab a bite."

His soulful, sweet smile sent her heart racing. Would she be able to concentrate?

"Sure," Jackie hoped she sounded casual.

"I could meet you back here or I can pick you up."

Then Jackie remembered. "I need to get home by 6 pm, I totally forgot. My mother is really wigged out these days by the press, so we've been eating in. I can't."

"No problem. I'm here if you need me," Josh stepped out.

Jackie was so confused. Was he asking her out? Or was he just being nice?

CHAPTER THIRTY-ONE

"I think I wet myself," Sophie's chins looked like a stack of pink donuts as she tried to avoid choking. It was a rare unscarfed moment.

Isabel crossed her arms and was furious. "I don't understand what's so funny."

"You sm…sm…" Sophie was wheezing. "Oh my god, I need to pee."

She struggled to get her round body out of the overstuffed blue velour chair.

"You better not have pissed on my chair," Isabel warned.

"Oh, that did it." Sophie grabbed herself and ran to the powder room closest to Isabel's family room.

Isabel got up and checked the chair cushion, rubbing a hand over its dry surface.

"Thank god," she sighed in relief.

Carmen refreshed the sangria pitcher with fruit, ice and more wine.

Isabel and Sophie had already polished off one and were working on the next when Isabel brought up funeral photographer. She thought her friend would find the idea of the photos touching, but instead, the bitch couldn't shut up about how hilarious she found them.

Sophie returned, breathing heavily. "Oh I feel better. Hey, Isabel, I think you should put that picture on your Christmas cards…" then she was losing it again. "Merry …Christ…mas, Zach's dead."

Carmen stared at Sophie. Isabel rolled her eyes at the maid and Carmen left the room.

"Even Carmen thinks you're being disrespectful." Isabel poured them each a fresh glass of sangria.

"I'm sorry," Sophie was finally catching her breath. "You have to promise you'll show me these pictures. If they are anything like what you described…"

"You won't see them," Isabel assured.

"Come on…" Sophie cajoled, raising her glass to Isabel. "Cheers! Maybe there's a beneficiary Zach forgot to change on one of his accounts."

"Oh, I hadn't thought of that," Isabel seemed pleased. "You've redeemed yourself."

Sophie shook her head. "Poor, Joanne."

"Indeed," now Isabel laughed.

"What's so funny," Jackie walked in, backpack in tow.

"We're just trying to get over all the sadness," Sophie lied and approached the teen. "You've been so strong."

"Joanne woke up today," Jackie wasn't really interested in their conversation, but she had tried to avoid interrupting them. "She recognized me… I think. I told her I'd be back tomorrow."

"Tell her hello from me," Sophie hugged Jackie. "I wish her well."

Isabel was thinking. "Did Dr. Wright say when she'd be released?"

"No," Jackie was surprised by her mother's question. "She hasn't even spoken yet, she just woke up. Besides, she'll need a lot of rehabilitation."

CHAPTER THIRTY-TWO

The phone trilled in the distance. Ken was almost out the door when he grabbed the call.

"Ken Avery, here."

"Here me out, don't hang up."

"Who is this?" Ken straightened a picture of his mother in the hallway.

"Collins."

Ken slammed the phone down.

The phone rang again.

"I'm not talking to you," Ken said and slammed the phone down.

The phone rang again.

"I had nothing to do with the shooting," Collins said before the phone slammed on him again.

The phone rang again.

Ken picked up. "I will get a restraining order if I have to. Do you understand?"

"I'm donating proceeds from my book to a scholarship in Zach's honor," Collins was quieter this time.

"Oh, so you do feel responsible for what happened," Ken retorted.

"Well, it's not what I did that got Joanne shot. It's what you did..."

"Don't you even try to turn this on me!" Ken hung up.

The phone rang again.

"Ken," Collins was calm. "I'm not trying to place blame, I'm trying to make amends. I wrote Joanne's Story for my own selfish reasons. But neither you nor I knew that lunatic was in line at that book signing."

Ken couldn't believe he was having this conversation.

"I visited Jackson in jail," Collins grinned to himself. "I felt really bad and wanted to get his side of the story."

"I'm sure you felt no such thing."

"I'm an opportunist, Ken. I won't lie. But I didn't incite a madman."

"Nor did I," Ken was ready to hang up.

"He saw your passion," Collins was even-toned. "Ken, he thought you were a protestor. He bought my book, never said a word to me at the signing. But once he read the book, he was convinced I was cashing in and you were righteous in your anger. You were there to remind everyone what a terrible person... what a terrible mother Joanne was, not the tortured Hollywood glamor queen he felt even I depicted her as... In his opinion, of course."

"I'm done." Ken hung up.

He was beginning to worry about Joanne's safety, and wondered if Collins had really seen Adrian Jackson.

CHAPTER THIRTY-THREE

Joanne wondered why her voice was weak. She couldn't speak well, or much at all. She understood that she had taken several bullets to her abdomen, lost a lot of blood and had swelling on her brain from a fall. But she couldn't remember much.

"Dr. Wright will be here to speak with you soon," a new nurse assured her.

A young woman came in and brought her fresh flowers. She was busy talking but Joanne couldn't concentrate on what she was saying. It was overwhelming. Joanne wanted to asked the woman to leave, but couldn't put the words together.

She closed her eyes. Hoping it would slow the woman down.

It worked. The talking stopped.

Joanne kept her eyes closed. This was comfortable. This is what she knew. The darkness was home. She could rest here.

"Is she asleep?" Another voice started.

"I think she's resting," the young woman said. "I just talked her ear off."

"Did she respond to you?"

"Not verbally," the woman said.

Joanne felt someone shaking her. She opened her eyes and looked at the two women, uncertain what they wanted.

"Joanne, how do you feel?" an older woman asked.

Joanne didn't speak. She felt this had to be the doctor; she was in a familiar white coat.

"Joanne, I would like you to try and say yes or no to my questions. Ok?" The doctor nodded, and Joanne found her hopeful smile encouraging.

Joanne nodded back.

"Do you know where you are?"

"No," Joanne managed.

"Do you recognize this young lady?"

Joanne looked at the younger woman again. "No."

Jackie's mouth flew open.

"I see." Then the doctor asked.,"Do you know who I am?"

"No."

Jackie panicked, "Maybe she isn't able to say, yes."

"Is there anyone you want to see?" Dr. Wright asked.

"Yes," Joanne said.

"Can you tell me who you'd like to see?"

"Ge..." Joanne struggled.

"Try it again, please," the doctor encouraged.

"Ge...ge..orge." A timid smile formed on Joanne's mouth.

Jackie turned away. She wasn't certain how to react or what she had expected. Why was she even at the hospital?

"I'm going to leave," Jackie muttered to Dr. Wright.

"It's going to take time, Jackie." The doctor grabbed her hand before she could rush out. "I'm here for you both."

CHAPTER THIRTY-FOUR

Collins returned to his rental house just after 10 pm. He was feeling better about Adrian Jackson having foiled his plans. Sure, he missed out on torturing Zach... but Zach wouldn't be around to protect Joanne, either. Sort of a fair trade.

Ken could fulfill certain torments Collins had devised for Joanne, and Collins could torture Ken in Zach's place. He hadn't even thought to include the stupid agent in his original plan, so he may actually be ahead of the game thanks to Jackson.

Collins quickly climbed the stairs to the rooftop terrace. He pulled out his binoculars and looked down at Isabel Manning's' house a few blocks away.

A familiar Mercedes rounded the corner and pulled into the driveway. One of the twin garage doors opened and the car drove in. No sooner was the car in than the door winked shut.

"Jackie's got wheels," Collins laughed. He saw a light go on in the living room and the maid pulling the drapes closed.

"You're welcome," he let the binoculars dangle around neck and uncapped the beer he had shoved in his pocket. "Well, daddy and Joanne aren't able to drive the Benz, so you just go right ahead baby girl."

He took a long swig of the brew and surveyed the neighborhood. He spotted a black SUV with a lone driver parked not far from Isabel's but straight in his line of vision. The tinted windows gave nothing away. It could be a hired car or someone spying on a cheating spouse. He raised his beer in a mock toast, he wasn't the only one working tonight.

He looked out at the millions of twinkling lights that made up the skyline of Los Angeles. "It's good to be home."

Isabel was in a mask of cold cream when Jackie got in.

"What's wrong? You look terrible and … is that pot I smell?" Isabel was scared for her, "You drove like this?"

She'd never seen Jackie high. The girl's eyes were half open. She was stumbling and she looked like maybe she had been attacked.

"Who did this to you? I'm going to call your fa…" Isabel stopped, realizing Zach wouldn't be there.

She sat down at the foot of the stairs, dumbfounded. She hadn't really missed Zach until now. Her sobs came softly.

Jackie squatted on the floor next to her, "It's about fucking time!"

Isabel didn't say anything. She looked at Jackie and saw Zach's eyes, his smile. She hadn't noticed how much Jackie was like her father … well, not in a long, long time.

"I was wondering if you'd ever show any real feelings. It hurts doesn't it?" Jackie raised her voice, "Were you ever real with him?"

"I loved your father," Isabel wept. "But we hurt each other… he never understood me."

Jackie didn't respond, just stared at her mother.

Isabel's laugh was quiet, sad. "I didn't understand him either."

"La-di-fucking-da," Jackie spat. "Spare me the memory lane. You can tell Lyle or Aunt Sophie your stories." Jackie rubbed her forehead. "I feel sick."

"Carmen, get Jackie some baking soda in water," Isabel called out.

"That was a big help…" Jackie covered her ears and pulled her legs in, rocking herself.

"What are you on?" Isabel asked calmly.

"I have no clue," Jackie laughed. "Marnie's pick… We knocked out a ½ pint of scotch and some of her pills."

"Pills?"

"Well, mother," Jackie was sarcastic. "Marnie's a pill thief. She goes through people's medicine cabinets and skims from whatever they have. She keeps a jar in her room. She likes to play 'Valley of the Dolls'."

"What?" Isabel was flabbergasted.

"She's always been obsessed with Sharon Tate and the Manson family murders, too. Her pill collection is huge now."

"Do her parents know?"

"Her mother knows. It's a pretty collection of colors and shapes… and since the jar keeps growing, she probably doesn't realize Marnie is taking any," Jackie reasoned.

"How many did you take?" Isabel thanked Carmen and handed Jackie the glass of bicarbonate and water.

Jackie slugged it and held her stomach. "Not many. I'm mainly drunk and stoned."

"We should go to the hospital," Isabel said.

"No fucking way. I hate hospitals!"

Jackie started to throw the glass, but Carmen ran over and grabbed it, "I get." The maid took the glass and left the mother and daughter to themselves.

"What is not many?" Isabel asked.

"Five, I'm too chicken to do more… Marnie likes to sample them and see how they make her feel. Who knows, I probably took an antibiotic, a laxative, one of her grandmother's nerve pills… I don't know," Jackie laughed.

"Marnie has a problem, Jackie."

"Really, you're one to talk." Jackie grabbed her stomach. It made a moaning noise.

"Have you eaten?"

"I don't know," Jackie shook her head matter-of-factly.

Isabel wanted to hug her, but knew better when her daughter was upset.

They both sat silent for several minutes. Isabel just watched Jackie, uncertain what to do.

"They're both gone." Jackie cried, "And I'm the only one that misses them."

Isabel's eye's got big. "Oh my God! Joanne died?"

"Worse," Jackie said.

"Worse than death?" Isabel couldn't imagine.

Jackie nodded.

"Wait, you mean… Oh my God… she was kidnapped from the hospital?" Isabel panicked, reaching for Jackie. "Carmen! Make sure the doors are locked. Call Mr. Lyle."

The teen stood and stepped back. "Joanne wasn't kidnapped. She just thinks she's… the old Joanne."

"Not again," Isabel said.

"Not again," Jackie mocked. "She doesn't remember anything about daddy, or her acting or anything."

"Please sit," Isabel tried to reason with Jackie. At least Joanne knew she was Joanne, right? "It's likely a matter of time before her memories catch up, Jackie. You told me the doctor had warned that it could be a slow process. I'm sorry I was insensitive."

That's what Zach would suggest Isabel do and she would finally try following his advice.

"Wow, the new, improved and understanding Isabel," Jackie swayed as she yelled.

"I want to make it up to you. I promise I'm not going to gossip and throw parties and be selfish anymore."

"I miss daddy so much and I was hoping Joanne would be normal and right now… Mother, you just don't matter." Jackie rubbed her watering eyes with both hands.

Isabel got up. "I deserve that. I'm going to change, Jackie. Can we hug?"

"No. You don't get to feel better." Jackie pushed past her and began ascending the stairs. "I'm moving on campus in a few weeks and don't worry, I'm not totally abandoning you."

Isabel put a hand to her mouth. The cold cream startled her. "Agh, I forgot I had this on."

Jackie kept walking up the stairs.

"Is that nec…" Isabel couldn't complete her sentence before Jackie cut her off.

"Yes, it's necessary, mother. We both have to grow up."

CHAPTER THIRTY-FIVE

Lou Bartalow dialed the number his assistant had given him. He knew calling Collins wouldn't amount to much, but he wanted to clear his own conscience. His pregnant wife and kids were out of town visiting her family for a month and the house was really empty. It made him feel empty.

He believed Collins was in on the Jackson hit. He didn't think the bastard would tell him anything, but he couldn't stop thinking about how upset Zach was about Collins' return, and the book. It was haunting him on a daily basis. Never mind the funeral! Seeing Jackie and Isabel only compounded his guilt.

Lou had never cared for Isabel. They were all friends in college and when he and Zach finished medical school, he was sure Zach would ditch Isabel. The woman was so unlikable. He couldn't understand what Zach saw in her, but figured they had a great sex life. That's what everyone thought in those days. She probably tied him up and fucked his brains out nightly. Or so they hoped, because anything less was just sad.

Jackie was such a good kid, though. She babysat, tutored Mexican children in English and played championship volley-ball. Not like the Sikes' kid Marnie, who was one step from turning tricks. Everyone worried Marnie would corrupt Jackie, but instead it seemed Jackie was the only thing keeping Marnie from going all the way over to the dark side.

He couldn't stand that Jackie was deprived of her father at such a pivotal age, but he couldn't figure out anything he could do to help. His plastic surgery practice had expanded to eight offices and he no longer was active in surgery, but instead ran the business, looked for investment opportunities and tried to be at home for meals with the family. Maybe he could offer to help Jackie with financial decisions regarding Zach's estate, but wondered if Zach might turn in his grave if Jackie had anything to do with him.

"Who is this…" a voice came from the receiver.

Lou was so lost in his thoughts that he had forgotten who he was calling.

Shit! Collins.

"Lou Bartalow."

"Son of a bitch," Collins sounded almost happy.

"You say it like we're old friends," Bartalow was perplexed.

"We are. Vasquez talked highly of you, Lou," Collins laughed. "I didn't learn about the whole Zach Manning connection until later."

"What exactly?"

"I know everything," Collins said. "I ghosted his fucking autobiography."

"About Zach."

"Tell you what, let's talk over a beer?"

"I could meet you somewhere," Bartalow offered.

"How about that steakhouse in Burbank, close to where you live."

Lou was now concerned. Collins knew where he lived, likely knew too much…

"Morton's bar in an hour," Lou hung up.

Collins was rather surprised Lou would choose such a public place, but at 3 pm on a weekday the crowd would be thin.

Lou was the first to arrive, and Collins figured it was best to let the bastard stew awhile.

He had a scotch on the rocks and watched the stock reports on the bar's TV. It was a good day on Wall Street and he really wished he could be more excited that his investments were seeing good returns.

It was quiet in the bar, but he wondered if a bus full of studio audience attendees would be piling into the restaurant in the next hour or so. It was hit or miss with the tourists. They were usually loud and worse than the paparazzi if a has-been movie star was eating in the restaurant.

Maybe he'd grab a steak if Collins left early and have his dinner at the bar. No reason to rush home... He caught his reflection in the mirrored bar display.

Christ, he looked like a fat bastard with a perm. His hair was always unruly and he never could seem to lose weight. He needed a haircut. His eyes looked puffy and he was growing thicker around the neck.

Then he saw an equally heavy Collins approaching in the mirror and he turned to face him, extending his hand.

Collins ignored the gesture.

"Had a little delay," Collins said as he mounted the barstool next to Lou and placed his motorcycle helmet on the next empty seat.

"No problem," Bartalow said.

"Been keeping up with Joanne, Isabel and the gang?" Collins laughed.

"Not sure I like the way you said that."

"Well, it's why we're here," Collins shrugged.

Lou stared ahead at the mirror.

"A screwdriver, on him." Collins pointed to Lou as he addressed the bartender.

Lou nodded to acknowledge he was buying.

The bartender poured the vodka and orange juice over ice and placed it in front of Collins. Collins still had his left pinky wrapped in white tape and held it out as he sipped on the cold beverage.

"What happened to your finger," Bartalow asked.

"Let's say," Collins drank a swig, then another... "...what is it about orange juice that makes you want to drink it fast?"

"Don't know. Your finger," Bartalow reiterated.

"It must be the vitamin c... anyway, I almost lost my finger." Collins gave Lou a cold stare, thinking about Colombia... then the more recent police interrogation.

"Ouch," Bartalow said. "Do you have any feeling in the finger?"

"I don't have much feeling. No," Collins said.

"What happened?"

"It's Joanne's fault. It happened the day she was shot."

Lou didn't say a word. He knew Collins was baiting him for a reaction and whatever he was going to share would likely be something Lou wouldn't want to hear.

"Let's get to the point," Collins said. "You called me."

Lou nodded acknowledgment, not sure what he was going to say or why he even agreed to meet the washed up reporter. "Fair enough. I don't really know why I wanted to talk to you. My friend is dead. His widow is still in the hospital. You wrote a book that upset my friend and incited Adrian Jackson to attack Joanne. I know you were cleared of any wrongdoing, but I don't trust you."

Collins motioned to the bartender to get him another screwdriver.

"I don't trust you either, Lou." Collins laughed, "You know, I wire tapped the Manning house and learned about Joanne's identity years ago. I admit that I gain information by any means necessary. But my stories are all true... well, to clarify, I fabricated a few to get my target's attention, but I'm honest about that."

Lou said nothing. His brow arched as he listened, watching Collins' reflection in the mirror.

"Adrian Jackson was going to hurt somebody and it happened to be Joanne." Collins continued, "My book, the 6 o'clock news or the next Star Wars movie could have set him off. But I have a question for you."

Lou still said nothing.

"I get that Zach wanted me out of the country and he wanted me to stop following Marquel, once I uncovered her identity as Joanne."

"By malicious means," Bartalow countered.

"I'm malicious?" Collins laughed. He took a long swig of his drink and motioned for the bartender to refill both his and Lou's drink.

Bartalow agreed.

"I even get that you make friends with drug lords. I know Vasquez needed to get his story written before he died... But you knew Vasquez was obsessed with the actress known as Marquel, and the series Suburban Life... You knew he wanted to meet her," Collins grinned. "And you knew he was a sick puppy."

Lou stayed quiet.

"If I hadn't come along, I get the feeling you would have sent Marquel and Zach to Colombia for a vacation."

Lou grit his teeth. His jaw pulsing.

"Maybe Zach wouldn't have returned. Maybe Marquel, excuse me, Joanne would have become a sex slave, or the next Mrs. Vasquez? You have a nerve calling me malicious."

Bartalow took a drink of his scotch.

Collins had him.

"You're the one playing with people's lives, Lou." Collins stood. "I just wanted to put their wretched stories in the tabloids for my own personal gain. But you called Zach Manning a friend! I wouldn't want to be your enemy."

With that, Collins picked up his helmet and left.

The bartender took Collins empty glass and wiped the bar.

"Can I get you anything else?" He asked Lou.

Lou was pissed. "Yeah, I'll have the porterhouse."

CHAPTER THIRTY-SIX

K en entered Joanne's room and found it empty. He wondered if he had made a wrong turn. He had a small vase of flowers for her and now he wished he'd put a card in. He wasn't sure she'd know they were from him without a card.

As he turned, Josh entered.

"She's having some tests done," Josh explained.

"Oh, I should come back then." Ken thought Josh was cute, perfect for Jackie.

"Have you talked with Dr. Wright?" Josh inquired.

"No."

"Joanne's having memory issues," Josh said.

"Oh God," Ken gasped. "Does she think she's Marquel again?"

"No, nothing like that," Josh answered.

"Then she has total amnesia?"

"Not exactly." Josh said, "I'm only telling you because I know how upset it made Jackie when she didn't recognize her. I'm not really supposed to share details like this."

"Josh, don't insult me."

"I'm not trying to insult you," Josh shut the door so they were alone inside the room.

"So what does Joanne... think happened?"

"She thinks she's in Shands Hospital in Florida, and she wants George to come and take her home."

"Oh God." Ken released the vase and the glass shattered on the floor. The long stemmed roses were tossed about like pickup sticks in shards of glass.

"I'll clean this," Josh said.

"I'm sorry." Ken went to get the trash can while Josh picked up some of the larger pieces of glass. "So she thinks she's still married to George?"

"No, she thinks they are dating," Josh replied.

CHAPTER THIRTY-SEVEN

JOZAC ATTACKER ADRIAN JACKSON HANGS HIMSELF Lou read the headline. One less lunatic to worry about.

He wondered if Collins had any intention of coming after him. What was it about the guilt he felt for Zach that made him want to contact Collins anyway?

If Zach hadn't asked for a favor just after Vasquez had, none of this would have happened. It just seemed perfect to Lou that Collins go to Bogotá, fulfilling both of his friends' requests. No one anticipated him coming back, why would they?

Lou wondered what it was that made him think he could somehow be loyal to everyone, sometimes to his own detriment.

Collins had a point. Why would anyone want to be his friend?

But Lou made sure everyone wanted to be his friend. He had always done that. Made up for his chubby unattractiveness with connections, favors, gifts, boob jobs—whatever it took.

Was there redemption for a guy who said yes to everyone?

Why the fuck did he need so much approval?

And why was he considering another meeting with Collins?

It was a sickness. He couldn't stand the man not liking him.

CHAPTER THIRTY-EIGHT

"Joanne, we're going to discuss what you remember," Dr. Wright said.

She had some of Joanne's clothing sent to the hospital. Though her patient would soon be released, it was uncertain where Joanne would be safest under the circumstances.

Joanne was cheerful. She had applied a little makeup, and looked more youthful with her hair down. She had braided a small strand on each side of her face.

They sat in chairs facing each other. Joanne's hospital room had been cleared of flowers and things that might distract her. Dr. Wright's hope was to jog the woman's memory in a way that would be transitional versus painful.

"I'm ready Dr. Wright." She smiled, "I look forward to going home soon."

"Where is home?" Dr. Wright asked.

"Gulf Hammock, like I told you before," Joanne laughed.

"Who do you live with?"

"My aunt."

"I want to do some word association, so just say the first thing that comes to mind."

"Ok," Joanne agreed.

"Dog."

"Cat," Joanne said.

"California."

"Hollywood," Joanne said.

"Black."

"White," Joanne said.

"George."

"Boyfriend."

"Girl."

"Boy, " Joanne said.

"Ken."

"Evan," Joanne said.

"Car."

"Truck," Joanne said.

"Pursuit."

"Car chase."

"Jackie."

"Kennedy," Joanne said.

"Zach."

"Man," Joanne said.

"Acting."

"Hollywood," Joanne said.

"Hunting."

"Fishing," Joanne said and laughed. "I was going to say George."

"PBS."

"Sesame Street," Joanne said.

"Marquel."

"I made that name up. Did George tell you?" Joanne asked.

"Marquel."

"Girl." Joanne grew quiet.

"Love."

"Hate," Joanne said.

"Letter."

"George," Joanne said, then looked confused. "I want to quit."

"What is it that makes you want to quit?" Dr. Wright asked.

"I don't know. I just have a bad feeling. My aunt used to say that when I have these feelings, I need to change to happy thoughts." Joanne began to fidget.

"Let's try happy thoughts." Dr. Wright said.

"I can't focus." Joanne got on her bed.

"When your aunt asked you to think happy thoughts, what was going on at that time?" Dr. Wright sat next to Joanne.

"My parents both died a few years apart. I would have times that I missed them. That's when I would try to think about the funny things that we did as a family." Joanne laughed.

"It's working." Dr. Wright smiled.

"But I just had a very bad feeling when I said George, after you said letter." Joanne sat up. "I don't understand why he hasn't been here to see me yet?"

"I'm going to change the subject a little. Ok?" Dr. Wright said.

Joanne nodded that it was ok.

"You know you are healing from gunshot wounds, correct?" Dr. Wright asked.

"Yes." Joanne affirmed.

"How do you think this happened?" Dr. Wright inquired.

"I don't remember," Joanne said. "But it must have been when George and I were in the woods. Right? I mean, that's the only time I'm… really around guns is when George takes me along on hunting days." Then her eyes got big. "Was he hurt, too?"

CHAPTER THIRTY-NINE

Isabel and Sophie strolled through Neiman-Marcus until they spotted the Chanel line. They were each looking for a gown to wear to the upcoming Famine Relief fundraiser. Isabel loved the designer, but was a little concerned about her finances.

"Let's try that boutique," Isabel spied a small store across the mall.

Sophie agreed and they moved on to the next store.

"I'm going to ask Lyle to marry me," Isabel told Sophie.

"He's never asked you?" Sophie stopped browsing and looked at her friend.

"Well, years ago, but it would've ended my alimony and I just figured now is the time." Isabel was very matter-of-fact. "I mean, I always thought I'd wait until Jackie's child support ended."

"Are you two still sleeping together?" Sophie asked.

"We do... not as often."

"You'd better propose when he's horny." Sophie was serious, "He needs to feel it was his idea. You have to get him hard as rock and wanting you badly."

"Wow," Isabel laughed. "When did you become a relationship expert?"

Sophie shook her head. "You're not getting any younger, Isabel. He's an entertainment lawyer. He represents actresses as well as filmmakers. You don't think girls negotiate with him?"

Isabel's eyes got big. "I hadn't thought of that."

"I'm really surprised."

Isabel was insulted.

"You didn't do the math, Isabel. Zach was never worth as much as Lyle. You were hanging onto an alimony check when you could have married and divorced Lyle for a mint!"

Isabel was stunned. She was so obsessed with controlling Zach's universe that she never thought of her own!

Sophie picked up a skimpy sequined gown that was cut down to the navel and rounded to the lower back. "Is Lyle attending the fundraiser with you?"

"Of course," Isabel said.

"Then you'd better wear this," Sophie handed her the dress.

"This is not me." Isabel held the garment in front of her.

"Exactly," Sophie said. "You have to surprise him. Remember the competition is stiff. I mean, you want to make him stiff."

Isabel muttered, "I can't let Jackie see me like this. She'd think I've lost my mind."

"Speaking of Jackie, is she sleeping with that hot male nurse yet?"

Sophie knew how to push Isabel's buttons.

"She's underage. I think he's smarter than that," Isabel snapped.

"Oh, you like him." Sophie was intrigued. "You want to ride that pony?"

"Stop. I'm not... He has been nice to Jackie and ..."

"And?" Sophie knew what Isabel was thinking.

"And I don't chase younger men, you do."

"Please, we both know better. The only difference is I can afford them, Mrs. Robinson." Sophie laughed.

"Well since you bring it up, would you loan me some money for this?" She held up the sequin gown.

"We'll consider it a wedding gift," Sophie winked.

Isabel giggled. "Yes!"

CHAPTER FORTY

D r. Wright entered the restaurant with her partner, Greta Goldberg. The couple were meeting with Ken and Evan to discuss Joanne's upcoming release and overall well-being.

They were both in white flowing caftans and ornate turquoise jewelry and resembled a mother daughter pair more than they did lovers.

Greta's newly cropped blonde pageboy framed her chiseled olive complexion. She was forever tan and rumored to be bisexual, but loyal to her committed relationships. Dr. Wright looked every inch the elegant, mature professional with her severely short gray cut. She never wore makeup, just lotion and lip gloss.

They dressed casual on weekends and often wore similar attire. It was their earth mother bond that brought them together, after all, and they refused to dress in suits when traveling or relaxing.

"Ken, Evan," Dr. Wright addressed the men, who were waiting near the hostess stand. "My partner, Greta."

Handshakes and air kisses were shared before they were led toward the reserved booth in the Beverly Hilton's restaurant.

"I'm famished," Greta caressed Judith Wright's forearm.

"We'll order some appetizers to get started, our treat," Ken offered.

The doctor turned to Ken, 'I'm sorry I didn't warn you ahead of time of Joanne's struggle with memory. Poor Jackie was so upset."

"I wish I could say I was surprised, but she's two for two. I just hope there are no more personalities waiting to pop out." Ken moved his silverware around and checked the salt and pepper shakers. He shook some salt in his right hand and tossed it over his left shoulder. Then he did the same with the pepper and laughed, "What the heck."

"Doesn't the pepper negate the luck of the salt?" Greta asked.

"Hell if I know. It's supposed to blind the devil, right?"

Dr. Wright laughed, "If you believe in the devil."

"Honey, I know there's a devil, because I was raised in Lubbock, Texas. The devil resides there." Ken fanned himself with his hand. "Homophobic hell."

Greta followed suit and began fanning herself like Ken, a gesture of camaraderie.

The doctor broke the moment and got back on topic. "It's not like a multiple personality disorder, Ken. She is stuck in a moment in time."

"Fugue, stuck, whatever you call it, I'm worn out." Ken sipped his water.

Evan listened, not wanting to jump into the conversation.

The doctor went on, "I don't think this state will last much longer, we did a word association and she had some answers that gave me hope that it's just a matter of time. I share this in the strictest confidence, of course."

Ken mimed zipping his lips. Again Greta mirrored his gesture, doing the same.

Dr. Wright seemed mildly annoyed with Greta's behavior. "Joanne and I were discussing George a lot in our last sessions and I encouraged her to write him a letter."

"A letter?" Ken was confused. "The man's dead."

Greta stifled a laugh. She liked Ken's playful nature, even if it was bordering on poor taste. It didn't hurt to have a sense of humor.

"It's a common practice, Ken," Dr. Wright explained. "You write a letter that you don't intend to send. It's a form of therapy that releases your mind from all the negative thoughts associated with the feelings you have toward someone who has hurt you."

Ken snapped his fingers. "Then I'm writing an epistle to Lubbock."

Greta snapped her fingers. "Oh, that's heavy, Ken."

The waiter took their appetizer and drink orders. Ken and Evan were sticking with water and the women were having wine.

"I have to release Joanne from the hospital soon and I was wondering if you would consider taking her in for a time." Dr. Wright looked first to Evan.

"Been there, done that," Ken said.

"She doesn't know us," Evan said. "We'd love to help, but we're not equipped to deal with her inevitable stress as memories resurface. It's not fair to us, or to Joanne."

Greta turned to her lover, "You said the same thing yourself. We'll take her in, ok? We have the guesthouse, and we'll work it out together."

Dr. Wright was touched by her partner's sincere offer.

"We'll be happy to see her as appropriate," Evan offered. "And I wouldn't rule out anything in the future, but I'm sure she could use a new start right now and, trust me, ours isn't the place for it."

"You're absolutely right," Dr. Wright agreed.

Ken turned to Evan, "You make our place sound awful."

"You know what I mean, the memories," Evan said.

"It was between our place and yours, Judith figured. And I'd love to help," Greta said to the men. "She's really a special soul to have survived so much."

Dr. Wright held up her wine glass and toasted, "to Joanne, and lasting friendships."

"Hear, hear," said Ken as he raised his glass.

CHAPTER FORTY-ONE

Joanne was dressed and packed when Dr. Wright entered her hospital room. She was nervous, but pleasant and busy writing in a notepad that the doctor had given her. Seated in an Indian squat in a chair, Joanne was jotting down anything that came to mind.

Her jean clad legs were crossed and resting against the chair arms. Her soft pink t-shirt gave her complexion a healthy glow. She looked renewed, at peace with everything the doctor had shared with her.

Joanne understood that she was in California, and that George wasn't in California. Dr. Wright told Joanne that she wasn't sure how she made it to California. This was true. No one had an accurate story from her past.

Dr. Wright shared that Joanne was at a seminar when she was shot and that the man who shot her was caught and later died while institutionalized.

Joanne trusted and believed the doctor. And since she didn't know anyone in town, she was grateful that the doctor and her partner would let her finish recovery in their home.

The doctor was concerned that things were moving forward a little too easily. She hadn't expected Joanne to accept and agree to her treatment plan. Her Plan B was to take Joanne to the home she shared with Zach and try to retrace their lives.

Collins had gotten wind of Joanne's condition from a hospital janitor who snitched in exchange for some much needed cash. The man even took some photos with a small pen camera Collins had supplied him.

The security guards that secured Joanne's room in the first weeks of her recovery were released from detail when Adrian Jackson was sent to a mental health facility. Joanne's lawyer protected his high profile client with a security guard and an approved visitor's list.

Collins couldn't get near the place.

His plan now was to see if she really had memory issues. He tipped off his paparazzi buddies so they would show up at the hospital for her departure. He also contacted a small but loyal *Suburban Life* fan club. He advised they bring signs and their autograph books.

Joanne was escorted in a wheelchair to a secured exit where she caught her first glimpse of a sign being waved outside. The letters were so big she could read it and it was obvious that the sign wavers were on the sidewalk, a distance from the exit door.

The first sign read:

We love you Joanne/Marquel!

She looked to Dr. Wright and was quiet.

Dr. Wright was caught off guard. She had no idea how these fans would know Joanne was leaving. Then she wondered if she'd just been oblivious to the fans. Were they out there every day?

Other signs read:

Joanne is back! So sorry about Zach!

Come back to *Suburban Life* Joanne!

We miss you, Joanne!

"Dr. Wright..." Joanne said. "Those signs that say Joanne... one says Marquel? I told you I thought up that name."

Dr. Wright turned the wheelchair around and headed back to the main hospital floor. "I'm sorry, Joanne. I've not shared enough with you."

"Where are we going?" Joanne was confused.

"I need to find a consult room." Dr. Wright moved quickly.

"Consult?" Joanne turned to look up at the doctor. "You look worried, like something is wrong."

"We need to have a serious talk."

"Haven't we been having serious talks?"

Dr. Wright stopped. "Yes, we have. But there's more."

"Are you leaving me here?" Joanne was worried. "You've been unable to contact my aunt…"

"No, I'm not leaving you. But you need to have a better understanding of the challenges you face." The doctor found a surgical waiting room and wheeled Joanne inside, closing the door. "I wanted to do this gradually and give you time to remember. So far, you've made some progress…"

"Some progress?" Joanne looked hurt.

The doctor sat on a chair opposite her patient. "You've made a *lot* of progress, Joanne."

Joanne looked confused.

"Those people holding signs are your fans. You have fans. Your name is Joanne Manning and your husband had a heart attack the day you were shot."

"Husband? No!" Joanne covered her mouth with her hand.

"The people outside know you as an actress. You were once on a television show called Suburban Life. Your stage name was Marquel." Dr. Wright knew this was too much too fast but she realized the world outside the hospital warranted that she tell her everything. Even the shelter of her own guesthouse wouldn't shield Joanne from the real world.

Joanne began to cry. "I don't know what you're talking about. Are you trying to trick me? Is this one of George's stupid jokes? He knew Marquel was one of my favorite names for…"

"I do not know George, other than the things you've shared with me."

"But you haven't told me where George is?"

Dr. Wright picked up the phone in the waiting area and dialed out. She had to let Greta know that things weren't going as planned.

Joanne got out of the wheelchair. "I want to go home. How do I get home?"

CHAPTER FORTY-TWO

Josh was coming in to work when he saw the small crowd of fans and wondered if Joanne had made it out yet.

He stopped to chat with the mostly female group. "Hey, did Joanne come out?"

"No!" One girl was frustrated. "I'm supposed to be at a class right now, but I wouldn't dream of missing this moment. They say she has amnesia again."

"Honestly, guys," Josh said, "if you really care about Joanne, you need to give her some space."

"Are you her doctor?" another girl asked. "You're cute."

Josh blushed. "No, I'm not her doctor. But I am concerned for her."

"So you know her!" The younger girls squealed and the small crowd drew in closer.

Josh looked at his watch, he was late for his shift.

"If she comes out, try not to frighten her," he told them.

Then he moved quickly for the door and went inside. Realizing how late he was, he took the hallway at a jog.

As he passed a surgical waiting room, he heard familiar voices and the name "Marquel" several times. He stopped, back-tracked to the room and knocked on the partly open door, pushing it open in the process.

Dr. Wright was on the phone and Joanne was on her feet, standing over the doctor. "I'm not leaving with you," Joanne's voice was raised.

"Joanne, are you okay?" Josh approached her.

She was relieved to see a familiar face and gave him a hug.

"Doctor Wright says I can't see George. I don't want to leave with her."

Dr. Wright hung up the phone and addressed Josh, "She's going to need a sedative."

"No I don't. I don't want to be drugged. I just want to go home," Joanne pleaded. She was frightened. "Please, Josh. Help me."

"Dr. Wright *is* helping you, Joanne. I know you can trust her because I trust her," Josh assured her. "In fact, if I were to need help she would be the first person I would consult."

A page for Dr. Wright was announced over the PA and she excused herself, knowing Josh would not leave Joanne alone. By the time she returned to the waiting room, Josh and Joanne were laughing and cheerful. She understood Joanne's trust of the young nurse, and she appreciated his presence and quick thinking.

"I'm going to see Joanne tomorrow, isn't that right, Dr. Wright? Or isn't that correct, Dr. Wright?" Josh asked.

Joanne laughed.

"Refresh my memory," Dr. Wright wasn't sure what he was concocting.

"I told Joanne I would come visit her tomorrow at your house," he nodded. "I mean, if that's okay with you, Doctor."

"Of course," Dr. Wright approved. "What time would you like to stop by?"

"Before my shift, say 3 pm?"

She pulled a prescription pad from her blazer pocket and wrote down her address.

Josh gave Joanne a hug. "If you see some people outside with signs, it's because they really like you. The young girls especially look up to you. We'll talk about it tomorrow."

Joanne returned the hug, "Thank you. See you tomorrow."

Then she turned to Dr. Wright, smiled and brushed aside a tear. "I'm ready, Dr. Wright."

CHAPTER FORTY-THREE

Collins kicked his motorcycle on and followed Greta Goldberg's black Jaguar sedan out of Cedars-Sinai parking lot. He could see all three women were in the car and he had traced the route to the doctor's home after following her several evenings. He had also scoped out some points where he could potentially watch the lesbians babysit the bitch.

The women lived in the Brentwood area in a Nuevo modern ranch home with no window coverings. The angles of the home, as well as the terrain of Sullivan Canyon, provided moderate privacy. The windows had reflective glass that kept out the sun's glare, but in the evenings it was easy to for him see inside.

The home had been renovated when the couple got together. They wanted a superb view and a large kitchen with colorful Spanish tile, olive wood cabinets and antique brass hardware. Many rooms resembled the clean, minimalist décor of the George O' Keeffe home they both admired. They had three large bedrooms and a guesthouse bungalow that Joanne would be able to stay in for as long as she needed.

The property also had a small pool dividing the two buildings which was intended for artist visitors, though it was often a drinking spot for stray coyotes. The couple didn't believe in chasing off the wildlife, rather they believed it was they who had encroached on nature.

The ranch home wasn't far from the hospital. The canyon was fast and easy for Collins on the motorcycle. He could get ahead of them and be in position to observe.

He sped past them.

Greta drove and Joanne sat in the front passenger seat. Dr. Wright wanted Joanne to see clearly where they were going while she would observe from her seat behind Greta.

Joanne pointed to a billboard. "Cellular phones are becoming so popular. I always thought pagers were advanced. Only doctors could have pagers when we were kids."

"You're right," Greta said. "I never really thought about it. I use a mobile phone," she opened her console and showed Joanne.

"That is so amazing," Joanne relaxed into her seat. "What do you do?"

Greta closed the console. "I'm a producer."

"Movie producer?" Joanne seemed impressed.

"Movies, some commercials…"

"I've always liked movies. Did you see that movie 'Ghost' with Patrick Swayze?"

"I have," Greta nodded. "It was very romantic, when they were spinning the clay."

"I know," Joanne agreed.

Dr. Wright was surprised at the ease Joanne had with this memory.

"Ghost seems like such an old term, doesn't it? I mean most people say spirit these days," Joanne rambled. "Pastors even say Holy Spirit, not Holy Ghost, unless it's an old time evangelist. Do you believe in ghosts?"

Greta caught her lover's eye in the rearview mirror and smiled. "Yes, I believe spirits are with us. What do you think Judy?"

"I'm not sure," Dr. Wright was sincere. "I've not encountered any, so I'm skeptical."

Joanne turned to face the doctor, surprised by her answer. "Haven't you ever wished you could speak with someone who passed on?"

That was the Joanne she had been waiting for.

"I've not felt the need. I was able to be with my parents, and even my grandparents, when they died. So I had closure," Dr. Wright explained.

"But don't you miss them?" Joanne asked. "I mean, wouldn't you like to see them or talk to them one more time?"

"That would be nice," Dr. Wright agreed. "But I'm not lonely. I have happy memories that I draw from, like your aunt taught you, so I never really miss them."

"Oh," Joanne turned back to the windshield. "Maybe once I remember things, I'll feel the way you do."

CHAPTER FORTY-FOUR

Jackie sat in a small café waiting for Charles Worthington.
The eatery catered to the UCLA student body and was sparse during summer. Now that Jackie had secured her housing arrangement, she was getting more familiar with the surroundings in her new neighborhood.

She had a full load of classes scheduled for the fall and decided not to walk for her high school graduation. It wouldn't be the same without her father, and she couldn't share the milestone with Joanne in her current situation. At least her mother was giving her space. In fact, she thought her mother was perhaps too anxious to get her out of the house since she latched on to the idea of marrying Lyle.

It was all hush-hush between her mother and Aunt Sophie about the pending nuptials. All Jackie knew for certain was that her mother wanted Lyle to fill the vacant spot she would leave when she moved out. Only Lyle hadn't asked yet.

"Aunt" Sophie threw Jackie a "college shower". She felt it was the least she could do since Jackie wouldn't be celebrating her high school graduation. It was a small event with just a few friends and their mothers, but it gave her some much needed hope and joy. It also got her new sheets, pillows, towels, dishes for four and small kitchen appliances.

With the extra cash she received from graduation cards Jackie would go thrift shopping for a desk, chair and dinette.

She was taking a twin bed from the guest room in her mother's house and a chest of drawers, but Isabel agreed to leave Jackie's bedroom intact.

Since Jackie needed the furniture, it gave Isabel an excuse to convert the guest bedroom to a workout room. She wanted to get toned for her upcoming wedding, after all.

Jackie sipped at her latte and read from Marnie's dog-eared copy of *Valley of the Dolls*. She'd never cared about the book before, but now that they were planning on being roommates, she felt it wise to understand Marnie's fixations. There was also the obsession with Sharon Tate and the film version of the novel, but Jackie figured she would just start with the book.

Charles Worthington walked into the café carrying a thin black satchel. He wore horn-rimmed sunglasses with lenses tinted a deep green, which he pushed on top of his bald head as he waved a cheerful hello to Jackie.

His shape and stature reminded her of Humpty Dumpty. He had a pleasant smile, pug nose and small, sharp eye teeth that were noticeable when he grinned.

He panted a little from his brisk walk into the eatery. His white button-up short sleeved shirt and black trousers looked freshly pressed, so she guessed she was his first appointment of the day. His black dress shoes shone and black socks peeked out when he his pants hiked up.

"I had a time trying to find parking. I wanted to avoid a meter," he was very thorough in the reasoning behind his actions. "So I circled several times before someone left and then I had to make sure I wasn't on the street-cleaning side."

Jackie nodded. "All she heard was parking... avoid meter..."

"Mind if I grab a joe?" Worthington asked. "It will only take a moment."

"No problem," Jackie said.

Worthington went up to the counter and dug his thick wallet from the back pocket of his trousers.

"Let's see. I might as well have a pastry, too," he talked to himself. He tapped on the countertop as he read the menu board. "Nope, I'll just have a black coffee."

The clerk poured his drink and gave Worthington change.

"For you kind sir," Worthington pushed a dime and nickel to the clerk. The kid nodded and placed the coins in his pocket.

Worthington walked slowly with the full cup. "I don't want to spill her."

Jackie wondered how long it would take him to get to the photos.

"Good coffee. Don't you think?" He asked Jackie as he placed his cup on the table, he had barely taken a sip.

She nodded. "I was curious. How did you get into this type of photography?"

His laugh was short and higher in pitch than his speaking voice. "It's always the first question. Not 'how are you Charles?' or 'what did you do this weekend?'"

"Well it's fascinating," Jackie countered.

Charles took a longer sip of coffee.

Jackie put down her book to be polite.

He tapped the table and muttered, "Okay, so the easiest way to put it is my mother died and I lived in one state and she was in another… so they buried her. They didn't wait to see if my father could afford to send me out to the funeral. Basically, my parents separated when I was a baby and my father kept me and my mother's family had a funeral without telling anyone."

"That's terrible," Jackie said.

"My grandparents didn't like my father. They let him take me not long after I was born, because they didn't want anything to do with him or his family. So they figured it was best for me to go with him and just cut ties."

"Why didn't they like your father or his family?"

Worthington took several more sips of his coffee. "He was an ex-con. Strong armed robbery and mother met him at a local diner where she waited tables. She found him exciting, given the people she grew up with," he shrugged.

"Now, I understand why you are a funeral photographer," Jackie said.

"Well let me clarify." Charles said. "My grandmother took photos of my mother at the wake. They were blurry and very poorly cropped. But she sent them to me, and that was my only communication with her family."

"Oh," Jackie wondered why Worthington's mother would accept her parents giving her baby away. It sounded unusual, but what did she know? She also hadn't experienced death before recently, so everything was weird and questionable.

Worthington moved his cup to the next table, preparing for the viewing.

"It was a custom in the rural community where my mother came from to take photos of the dead, and I just wanted to become a resource, so others like me would have a quality memory," Worthington added a solid tap to punctuate his statement. "Shall we?"

Jackie nodded and moved her cup and book.

Worthington brought out a small table-top easel. He placed the photos on it, which were still covered with a black velvet cloth. "I would normally do this in a private home, but given there aren't any patrons in our section, I feel you'll have adequate privacy. Let me know when you are ready."

Jackie nodded.

Worthington lifted the veil on the photos and revealed the first black and white image—a photo of Isabel with her hand on Jackie's waist. It captured them from the back as they looked at Zach, who was blocked by the women, with the exception of his hairline and the top of the casket. The lighting was intimate.

Jackie gasped, her eyes welling with fresh tears.

"That's the most beautiful photo I've ever seen," she almost didn't want to see any others. It gave her a feeling of completion. The photo showed her mother as she had always hoped her to be, caring and supportive, while her father rested, respected and loved.

She was beginning to understand this odd little man.

"Let me know when you would like to see the next photo," Worthington said.

"I'm ready."

He showed her the photo of her father's hands.

She couldn't speak. Her eyes spilled big droplets.

Worthington handed her a pocket size package of tissues.

"You really come prepared," she smiled through her tears.

He smiled back.

"I'm so glad they're black and white," Jackie complimented him. "These are a like looking at a daydream."

When he got to the photo that Isabel posed for, it was cropped to show Isabel's slim figure from the waist down only, with her hand on Jackie's slightly out of focus and Zach resting, in focus.

"This is brilliant," Jackie whispered. She was less mournful and more in awe of the man's genius. "My mother will demand to see the uncropped version."

"It's not cropped. This is how I shot it," Worthington was serious.

"Really." Jackie placed a hand on his. "Then my father is truly resting in peace, Mr. Worthington. You honored him as he would have wanted. I can't thank you enough."

He slid the photos into a decorative sleeve and gave them to Jackie, along with a white envelope. "You can mail the balance when the life insurance check comes in, if need be."

Jackie wasn't used to paying bills, "I will find out about that. This is very new to me."

"I understand," Worthington said. "By the way, are you con-sidering becoming a writer?"

"Ah, oh, no." Jackie was surprised by the query. "Why do you ask?"

He pointed to the book.

"That, my dear, that was her first novel, and her name was Jacqueline as well. It looks like a well-studied copy, so I thought you were considering writing a breakout novel," he smiled. "That novel was a first of its kind."

"Oh, well, my best friend is obsessed with Sharon Tate and she was in the movie version…"

"Well, I think it was unfortunate that Sharon Tate became famous for dying a horrible death," Worthington said. "Now there is a woman that I would like to have photographed."

Jackie's eyes got big.

"You are thinking of the murder, but I am speaking to her final rest," Worthington clarified, indicating the package of photos he had just given Jackie. "You mentioned that these photos would give your father a final rest. If I were to do the same for someone who had suffered as she had, by showing her resting, beautiful… then it might help negate the violence that befell her and her unborn child."

"Oh." Jackie was a little overwhelmed by the discussion.

"What are you majoring in?" The photographer seemed comfortable changing subjects.

"I don't know. I'm just trying to get my general education classes out of the way while I figure it out," Jackie answered.

"Well, you'll find your inspiration," Worthington was positive. "If you need any more copies of the photos please let me know. The negatives are secure. You have the only prints."

Jackie's thoughts were all over the map, between her father's funeral photos, and now Marnie and the Sharon Tate murder. It seemed that life and death were a blend of the beautiful and the morbid.

Then she thought about Joanne, and how she fit into this same imagery.

CHAPTER FORTY-FIVE

Collins could see little of the women as they moved about in the Wright/Goldberg home. Disappointed that the perch he chose didn't provide enough visibility, he decided to return home and plan a rendezvous with Joanne once the doctor and her partner were out for the day.

He drove quickly and was nearly clipped by a black SUV that pulled out of nowhere. The vehicle swerved around him. Collins couldn't process where it came from, it happened so fast. He had to pull over for a moment just to get his head together. Where were the LAPD when you needed them?

The house he rented in Isabel's neighborhood had just enough furniture. Anything more would be a distraction. Collins stripped down to his black briefs and opened a beer. He caught his reflection in the sliding glass door that led to a balcony.

His paunch made him look uncomfortable. In fact, he was uncomfortable bending. It was as though his skin were pulled taut in the middle. He needed to lose weight, but he really didn't care about his looks anymore. He'd once cared, before he left for Colombia, but that experience had aged him and he no longer wanted the things he once had.

He also hadn't been with a woman that he desired in a long time, so he saw no reason to groom or attempt to make himself attractive. He was no longer sure he could love or care for another individual.

Vasquez had provided him sexual services via the women he had trafficked to South America. The girls were mostly Mexican, but there were a few blondes that were abducted in Germany and the U.S. All the girls begged to go home when they weren't drugged to the point that communication was impossible. The Mexican girls were somewhat less resistant, and because they spoke the language many enjoyed a better quality of life as a result of their cooperation.

At first Collins enjoyed the occasional orgy. Then Humberto Vasquez joined Collins and the women. Soon Collins found himself uncomfortable with the younger Vasquez's attention and began refusing the offer of sexual favors.

Some of the women thought Collins would help them escape, but he never had much empathy for them. Empathy would weaken him, and the slaves were a constant reminder of how trapped he was. He wouldn't allow himself to get emotionally involved, lest the cartel decide to teach him a lesson, a lesson that would inevitably bring harm to the girls. Instead he kept his distance.

There wasn't anyone to comfort Collins, aside from Humberto, whom Collins tried to avoid. Humberto's ailing father was entertained by Collins' stories of Marquel during breaks from the writing process. Collins played jester to the older man's kingship in order to avoid Humberto and the women in his downtime. He embellished so much about his time with Marquel that he almost began to believe his own lies.

He told Vasquez he had a sexual encounter with the actress when he was stalking her. He said he had been watching her skinny dip in the pool and boldly jumped the fence and began photographing her. She didn't resist and posed for him. Then she taunted him to take off his clothes and join her. From there he told Vasquez how he took her in the pool and on the deck, just before her lover got home. The story was so preposterous that

Vasquez asked him to retell it many times, like a child demanding the same tremendous bedtime story.

To gain Collins cooperation, Vasquez convinced the younger man that a six-figure check awaited him once he completed his ghost-written autobiography. He explained that Collins' abduction had been necessary, as he saw no other way to hire a biographer.

Collins agreed to cooperate, but it wasn't a matter of choice. He knew he had everything to lose and as such he would do nothing less than his best, given it could be his last work.

Collins only wished he could have helped the women who were abducted in much the same way he was. He knew they would never see their families again. Hell, he didn't have any family to return to, just his colleagues in the press. He felt at times that it would be better to die than be used, but trusted the older Vasquez to be a man of his word.

He still wondered why the women didn't band together and blindside the cartel when they had their pants down.

Josh stopped by to see Joanne as promised. He didn't have a plan, but wanted to honor his commitment to her. They made tea and tried to work through a clumsy conversation that was mostly focused on Josh's interests.

He knew Joanne was working with Dr. Wright on her memories and he was uncertain what to discuss, so he rambled about the hospital and his schedule and little else. He didn't want to bring up Jackie for fear it would begin a dialogue he wouldn't know how to back out of.

CHAPTER FORTY-SIX

Ken and Evan stopped in Trader Joe's to pick up a few things for dinner. They were in the produce isle when they spotted Lou Bartalow handling a shitake mushroom.

Ken approached, pointing to the sign. "Feeling like *shit?*"

Lou's train of thought derailed and he looked up. "Huh?"

"It's Ken," Avery put a hand on Bartalow's arm. "How have you been?"

Bartalow laughed, "I just got what you said … I thought you were someone else."

"Well who doesn't feel like shit these days," Avery said. "But really, shitakes are a Chinese symbol for longevity. I once had a crush on Bruce Lee and started learning all things Chinese. I mean, the man had been dead awhile… Anyway, don't let the *shit* fool you."

The jokes weren't working for Lou, but the longevity part was good to know.

Evan reached out his hand, "Evan, we met at Zach Manning's wake."

"Right," Bartalow nodded. "I guess you're right, Ken. I guess we're all feeling like shit under the circumstances."

"Guess you've been spared the Mark Collins' calls," Avery lamented. "He's on my last nerve."

Bartalow didn't respond.

"Did you two ever meet?"

"I know of him," Bartalow stretched the truth, "I mean, who doesn't, right?"

Ken laughed. "You have a point. Well just be glad you don't have anything to do with him. He is relentless."

"In what way?" Bartalow asked.

"He wants to wrap me in his web of lies and I'm not going to let that happen," Avery moved out of the way of a shopper's cart. He noticed some plums in the passing basket and mouthed to Evan to remember plums.

"Web of lies?" Bartalow repeated.

"It's a long story and I'd be happy to tell you another time, but our frozen foods need to get home soon," Ken pulled a business card out of his wallet and gave it to Bartalow.

"Have you seen, Joanne?" Bartalow asked.

Evan gave Ken a look. He hoped his lover wasn't going to say much.

"She looks good," Ken nodded. "We really have to go."

Bartalow knew by their behavior there was something going on, but maybe it was best he didn't know. If he stayed out of the fray he could forget his involvement. But then he thought about Avery's comment regarding Collins being relentless.

"Tell her hello," Bartalow said.

"Thanks, we will." Evan commandeered Ken to the plums.

Bartalow watched the two. He knew they were hiding something, and of course Avery would know more about Joanne than anyone, other than perhaps Jackie. He had to stop thinking about all of this shit and just get back to his office.

Isabel admired herself in the teal sequined gown. She had to forgo any undergarments as the lines would show.

She was proud of herself. She had shed fifteen pounds on the pineapple diet and had a glowing bronze tan. She had also spent a week at an exclusive spa where she could sunbathe nude and have her bikini line waxed and shaped to impress Lyle.

She so enjoyed pampering.

She couldn't imagine Zach ever having been up for anything sexually adventurous and wondered what Joanne saw in him.

Zach had always been a considerate lover, and in their younger days he had plenty of stamina, but then again, she thought about Lyle's habits. He could fall asleep snoring immediately after a climax...

Oh well, she just needed to get him to agree to marriage.

Her hair was in a perfect chignon and she wore long droplet faux diamond earrings and no necklace, as she wanted her breasts and navel to be the center of Lyle's attention. She turned to observe herself through the mirror on the opposite wall and saw the dip in her dress was resting right above the crack in her ass.

What would she do if the room was cold, she wondered? She could throw Lyle's jacket over herself, which would look kind of sexy, sweet... and chivalrous. She pulled a white pashmina out of a drawer and draped it over herself. It looked too heavy and the white too stark against her skin and the teal dress. Why hadn't she thought about this earlier?

The doorbell rang and she knew it was Lyle. Carmen would have to let him in.

The phone also rang, surprising her. She grabbed the line by her bed, "Isabel Manning"

"Listen, I can't make it," Sophie coughed. "I have strep. Let me know how it goes."

"You sound terrible." Carmen knocked at Isabel's bedroom door, she turned to shoo her out. "Tell Lyle I'm coming soon."

Lyle pushed the door open and saw Isabel. He was taken aback.

"I have to go," Isabel hung up on Sophie.

She took in his elaborate Indian garments as Carmen backed out of the room. A regal, long coat of red and black embellished brocade with silky black pants, his feet sandaled.

His silver hair was trimmed without sideburns and he had a windblown look where his part was mussed a bit, making him look sexy... and cute. His woodsy pine cologne filled the room and she realized she hadn't put on any perfume.

"Is that your harem girl look?" he asked, touching her navel. "You need a jewel here."

She gasped a little. "What do you call this jacket?"

"It's a Sherwani, do you like it?" He tipped her chin upward to give her a light kiss.

She returned the kiss. "You look handsome. But what made you decide to where this?"

Lyle seemed puzzled by her question, "The theme. Arabian Nights."

"Theme." She pulled back and looked at herself. "I didn't even pay attention. Do you think this will be okay?"

Lyle stood behind her and they gazed into the mirror together. "I guess we should have coordinated colors. Do you think the teal and red clash?"

They seemed taken with their look. She noticed his hair again, and the way he carried himself... even the way he kissed her.

He was sleeping with someone else! His confidence was not her Lyle.

"Lyle," she cooed. "I have no undergarments on because the lines would show…"

His eyes lit up, "Naughty girl."

She lifted her dress to show him her newly trimmed look.

"Oh my God," he said.

"Too bad we're pressed for time." Done with the sneak peek, she dropped the hem of her dress.

"Let me have another look."

"We could… but I can't mess up my hair," she purred.

She wanted to get to the business of proposing, but there was more than one road leading to the subject.

"I guess if I got on top," she pushed the thin straps off each shoulder and let the dress fall to the floor. She was fully exposed, clothed only in her earrings.

He slipped his pants off, already erect. She unbuttoned his jacket slowly as his hands roamed all over her. She knew he was watching her ass in the mirror, and she knew she looked great.

"I can't wait," he pleaded.

She would make him. She intentionally took her time with the last few clasps.

"Lie down on the bed," Isabel instructed.

"God, you've changed."

She slipped atop him and he groaned. His hands moved over her breasts and then to her hips as he guided her in the need for speed. She moved slowly at first and then felt her own want for satisfaction. In the heat of the moment her earrings beat the sides of her neck and she said, "Marry me, Lyle. Say, yes."

He didn't care, "Yes, yes, yes, yes, yes…"

She rode him hard, until they were both in a 'yes' unison of pleasure and climax. She lingered there awhile longer and then rolled over and rested next to him.

They were both limbered and happy. She giggled.

"It was good, right." He was pleased with their performances.

She placed her hand under her cheek as she propped herself up on one elbow. "I love you, Lyle," she ran her fingers over his chest.

He looked up. "That was wonderful."

"Well, we'll do this more often once we tie the knot."

"You're serious?" he asked.

"Of course, I'll be Mrs. Lyle Herlbert and we'll be living together …"

He stopped her, rolling to face her. "Isabel, are you sure you're over Zach's death? This is very radical for you."

She was confused. "Over?"

"Why else would you behave like this now? I mean, think about it, Isabel. You turned me down years ago and I knew you always loved him. You wanted to wait and have this open relationship. We had fun," he placed a finger over her lips before she could speak.

She sat up. "Lyle, I'm ready."

"I'm going to be honest, I'm not sure I am." He sat up beside her.

They looked at their naked selves in the mirror. Her makeup was bit smudged, her hair tousled.

"Besides, you'd have to agree to a prenuptial if we were to marry," Lyle was candid.

"Why? You have no children to protect."

"Isabel, you have never been in love with me. We have a great time, but I run the risk of you finding someone who means as much to you as Zach, and then you'll divorce me and want alimony. I have to protect myself." He wasn't going to play games.

"But you love me," Isabel said.

"Yes, I do, but you also drove me away. You wanted to date others, so I've dated others... and I could marry any of those women."

"Would you have wanted a prenuptial when you first asked me?"

He laughed. "Not likely, I was head over heels in love with you and would have followed my heart."

She took a deep breath, "Let's clean up and get to the party. I need to find someone to marry."

"An arrow to the heart," Lyle said. "You could still live a good life as my wife. I'll give you a generous shopping allowance."

"No, I'll keep you as my lover. You can screw me when my rich 90-year-old husband is asleep," she laughed and turned away. Hot tears were beginning to well up and she didn't want her mascara to run.

Lyle and Isabel were one of the most photographed couples at the gala. Isabel's revealing dress showed up in the trades as "mourning attire." A story that had a strange parallel with Lyle's accusation that Isabel had never quite gotten over Zach.

Though Zach had passed months earlier and their marriage had been over for years, Isabel was skewered by some talk show hosts and outspoken comedians as a woman on the prowl. They couldn't find Joanne and it was a slow news cycle, so Isabel rated higher on the LA social register.

"God, Isabel," Sophie was in approval mode. "You don't need Lyle now."

Her friend subscribed to everything Hollywood and fanned out the publications on her patio table for Isabel to review.

They toasted each other with their mimosas.

"There are only great photos, I'm shocked!" Isabel gushed.

"That's not a mistake. You're getting public support for a new sexy image, and the mourning story stuck, so the press wants to beat that horse," Sophie poured herself another glass.

"Who knew?" Isabel was pleased. "Zach would never have approved."

Sophie laughed. "Lyle may think twice about the prenup! If you keep this kind of press up you're great for his image."

"Oh," Isabel mentioned as an afterthought, "I was offered a chance to guest host an episode of a new program that E! is starting on celebrity divorce. Can you imagine?"

"Really!"

"Yes and I turned them down, for Jackie's sake."

"Well, it's a little late for the divorce story," Sophie agreed. "But brilliant thinking by the producer! I mean Zach isn't here to defend himself, you'd rule the roost."

"Is it evil that I really wanted to do the show?" Isabel questioned.

"I'd believe you were sick if didn't want to."

CHAPTER FORTY-SEVEN

Collins left his motorcycle parked down the street and walked up to Dr. Wright's home. He had seen both cars leave at different intervals and they didn't have a passenger. Now was his chance to taunt Joanne.

He wanted to catch her off guard. Mess with her mind.

The walk was a little more challenging than he had anticipated. His knees were creaking and he was nearly out of breath when he got to the top of the driveway.

Everything was quiet. The patio that led to the pool was open and unfenced. It looked like a sheet of blue glass. The deck had unfinished log chairs and tiled nesting tables scattered about.

"Can I help you?"

He heard someone behind him. It startled him.

"Oh, I was," he said as he turned to look right into her innocent face. "I'm looking for Joanne."

"I'm Joanne." She smiled, clearly not recognizing him.

It was so bizarre that she didn't have a clue who he was.

"I'm…" He had to think quickly, "I'm Ken Avery."

"Nice to meet you Ken," Joanne said. "Why are you looking for me?"

"I used to represent you and I'm hoping that once you recover fully, you'll want to come back to work," Collins answered.

Her mood changed, she began to fidget. "I'm not looking for work at this time."

She was now uncomfortable with him.

"I understand. How about I come by tomorrow and take you to lunch? We could visit a little and I could show you around the area."

"I suppose that would be ok, given our past," she agreed after a pause.

"Yes," Collins repeated. "Given our past, we really should spend some time together."

CHAPTER FORTY-EIGHT

Josh and Jackie entered the thrift store and headed for the furniture section. They had already been to five stores and it was taking all day to get from one place to the next between traffic and parking challenges.

A frayed recliner attracted Josh. "I'm going to steal this baby if you don't snap it up."

"Go right ahead." Jackie moved toward a bistro set, "This is perfect."

"It only has two chairs," Josh complained. "How are all three of us going to have pizza on that?"

"You'll have to sit on the floor while Marnie and I sit at the table. Besides, when does a busy hospital nurse find time to freeload with college students?"

"Freeload? I believe I'm the one who can afford to dine out... and I'm getting this recliner," he pushed back in the seat. "I'm serious. This is the perfect football chair."

Jackie ignored him, pushing on the table to check its stability. The chairs were sweetheart designed in white iron and the table top was a similar design with a glass inset. "I'm going to get a clerk to tag this. I still need to find a desk."

"I have a card table you can use. It's also my dining table, so that means I'll have to eat on the floor at my place *and* your place." He closed his eyes and relaxed.

"I thought you could afford things. Why do you have a card table for your dining table?"

"I'm a guy. I don't need anything fancy."

"I'll wake you before I leave," Jackie walked away.

She found the housewares section and puttered around. She picked up a large mixing bowl, a few cookie sheets and a knife sharpener.

She remembered her mother telling Carmen to sharpen the steak knives before one of her parties. Carmen was confused and her mother explained that just about any knife used frequently needed to be sharpened from time to time. Jackie had already received a new butcher block with kitchen knives for a gift, so now she could maintain them.

Josh was snoring by the time she returned. He had worked a double shift, but still insisted on helping her shop. She plopped herself down in an overstuffed chair next to him, placing her shopping basket on the floor while she reviewed her check list.

"Ma'am," a young male clerk approached. "You and your husband need to check out. We're closing in 15 minutes."

"He's not," she laughed, "I have the dinette and these items. I'll be up in a moment."

She shook Josh and he jumped, "Where am I?" He grabbed the arms of the recliner.

"You're snoring," Jackie said. "They want us to pay for our purchases. They're closing."

"Oh, I'm so tired," Josh mumbled and stretched. "How bad was my snoring?"

"Loud enough that they heard you in the back room and complained." She laughed, "Just kidding, it was a quiet growl, like a bear cub."

He rubbed his eyes. "I think you're flirting with me... again."

"We need to get moving." She stood, "Can we fit the recliner and dinette in your van?"

"I'm not getting the recliner," he laughed. "I was just checking your tolerance for guy furniture and you passed."

"Huh?"

"Well, you weren't put off by a beat up recliner. You didn't even flinch, so I think we can move on to the next stage of our courtship."

"Courtship?" She blushed.

"We're already shopping for furniture and we haven't even been on a date," he got down on one knee. "Would you like to go to Jack-in-the-Box for dinner?"

She pushed his forehead. "In-N-Out Burger and you're on."

"A burger connoisseur, I'm impressed," he kissed her hand. "Only the best for you, my lady."

She rolled her eyes.

They fit the dinette into his minivan after folding down the seats and wedging the chairs together.

"I thought only married people with kids drove these," Jackie teased. "I mean, you are a single guy... aren't you?"

He started the vehicle and they headed to the In-N-Out. "I'm not married, Jackie, and it's good to know you have standards. You shouldn't date married men."

"So why do you have this van?" She didn't take anything he said seriously.

"Well, I lived in it for awhile. My grandparents traveled the U.S. with this van. It has over 200,000 miles and once they saw all they cared to see, they gave it to me. When I first started working at the hospital, I didn't have an apartment, so I lived in my van until I saved enough for first and last month's rent, you know the drill."

"So where do you live?" Jackie realized she had only seen him at the hospital, the wake and now her place.

"Now I'm hurt." He put a hand on his heart. "You just don't listen. We had a moment I thought, and now I can see you were only paying attention to this," he motioned to his body.

"Please, you've never told me where you live."

"Okay, since you're listening," Josh returned both hands to the steering wheel. "I live in Westwood."

They arrived at the drive-through and Jackie reviewed the menu. "I heard. Westwood... I'll have..."

They placed their order and ate in the van. When they were finished he drove her to her apartment and helped set up the dinette. He kissed her on top of her head before he left and reminded her to keep her doors locked.

Jackie was confused by his kiss. "Are you doing this because you promised my dad you'd look out for me."

"Yes and no," Josh answered. "I am honoring my word to Zach, but I also like you. We have fun."

She walked him to his van. "So am I supposed to think of you as a big brother?"

"I hope not," he bent down and kissed her, his tongue lingering in her mouth this time.

She wrapped her arms around his shoulders and he pulled her in tight about the waist. She didn't want to stop.

"Let's go back inside," she said.

"You're seventeen." He pulled back, "I respect you, and your father, and we'll wait."

"Let's go for a drive," Jackie insisted.

"Let's go for a walk," Josh said. "Let's take it slow."

"No, I'd rather make out right here." She reached up to his mouth and wrapped her arms around him again.

They were lost in a moment of passionate kisses when a car drove by and honked, startling them both. There were whistles and catcalls that embarrassed her, but he found them flattering.

"They all want to be me," he whispered in her ear.

Her heart lept. She didn't know how she was going to survive until her eighteenth birthday, which wasn't until January.

CHAPTER FORTY-NINE

Joanne lounged at the edge of the pool. She wore cut off jean shorts and her shirt was tied up under her bra line.

"Ellie May Clampett?" Greta approached Joanne with a glass bottle of water.

"Oh," Joanne laughed, "I remember that show. And this is a see-ment pond. The Beverly Hillbillies. Oh my gosh and I am in California. This is too funny."

Greta sat next to Joanne and rolled up her slacks, putting her feet in the water. "We're making pizza in a bit. We can all personalize our own. It will be fun."

Joanne smiled. "Sounds good."

"We have to give the stone oven a workout now and then."

Joanne hesitated before saying, "I would be happy to do your housekeeping. I feel I need to do something to help out."

"We'll figure something out, but we can't let our housekeeper go, she has a family to support."

"That's very considerate."

"We believe in supporting women with a living wage. And if we can hire a qualified woman, we do. We want to help women in need."

"Can I ask you a question," Joanne felt a little awkward.

"Sure."

"When did you know you were different?"

"You mean a lesbian?"

"Yeah."

"As a young child, but I didn't really tell anyone or share it with family until I was out of college," Greta took a sip of her water.

"What did your parents think?"

"Funny, they knew all along. They were just waiting for me to feel comfortable with myself." Greta laughed.

"Really," Joanne said. "To think that they knew you better than you knew yourself."

"Humph, funny how that works." Greta splashed her feet.

"You both seem very happy," Joanne reflected.

"We are. We met at a networking function and I fell in love with Judith's brilliance. She's actually older than my mother. Which didn't go over well with my grandmother, of all people."

"Really."

"Yes, my grandmother is very protective and while she accepts me for who I am, she really wanted me to find a younger *Jewish* lesbian to be my girlfriend."

They both laughed.

"Oh, before I forget," Joanne said, "a man named Ken came by and asked to take me to lunch. He said we know each other. Well, he said… under the circumstances, no… given our past we should spend some time together." Joanne smiled.

"Ken! I think he is so fun. Maybe we should all do lunch." Greta said, "I mean you, me and Ken. Judith doesn't get his humor."

"So you approve?" Joanne asked. "I wasn't sure if I should go."

"By all means, and throw some salt over your shoulder if he says something you don't like. He'll think you are a kindred soul."

CHAPTER FIFTY

Lou Bartalow's pregnant wife Suzy was now bedridden at her mother's home.

She called him, crying that she had gone to the ER in Denver for spotting and the doctors put her on bed rest for the remainder of her pregnancy. She wasn't certain she was going to get home until after the baby was born. Her family was happy to take care of her and the grandchildren, but Suzy missed Lou and their home. The kids also missed him and she wanted him to come out and spend time with them.

He reassured her he would come out within another week or two. For now it was like a gift to be alone while he was monitoring Collins' every move. He had called a private investigator friend, Rick Jones, and had his service follow Mark Collins.

So far Jones had revealed that Collins was in a rental house near Isabel and Jackie.

That pissed off Lou. He felt the scumbag Collins would definitely go after the women now that Zach was gone.

Jones would enlist the help of his elite team: Clark Roberts, Bart Petty and Dane Blacksmith.

This was the least Lou could do for Zach. He would make it up to his deceased friend by having Collins' watched—the stalker stalked.

Lou would make certain nothing happened to the women. He was less worried about Joanne after learning she was under a doctor's care. It was obvious from Collins' proximity to Jackie and Isabel that they were his immediate target.

Collins posted a new pin in the map on his wall. He had all the landmarks from recent events pinned.

There was Isabel's home, Zach's former home with Joanne, his multiple bookstore signings, the hotel where the seminar took place, the hospital, the police station, and the prison where he visited Adrian Jackson before he was moved to the institution where he killed himself. There was also the Burbank restaurant where he met up with Bartalow, the home of Dr. Wright, and a star marking where the Hollywood sign stood.

He hadn't accomplished that one yet.

He posted some new photos of Joanne on his wall. He had hundreds, in addition to pictures of George, Zach, Jackie, Isabel and the baby girl, Marquel.

Adrian Jackson may have slowed his progress, but he certainly didn't hinder it. This was shaping up even better than he had anticipated.

CHAPTER FIFTY-ONE

Jackie spent her first night alone in the new apartment. Marnie hadn't quite moved in completely and it was a final chance for Isabel to let go.

Isabel and Sophie brought pizza and reminisced about their own college days. Jackie was a little surprised at her mother's admissions to sneaking boys in and the parties the women had. It was almost a license for Jackie to follow in her mother's footsteps, but Jackie wasn't as bold.

The older women were enjoying the pizza party on the college campus a little more than Jackie had expected, and she felt sort of like she was the guest in their apartment. But it was one of the more relaxed times she shared with her mother. For that she was grateful. Even if she was still getting used to her mother's recent weight loss and changes in hairstyle and clothing. Her mother wore her brunette hair down with a long side bang and had added jeans and casual knit pullovers to her wardrobe.

Isabel was open with Jackie about her new outlook on finding a husband. She wanted someone who would include her in his work. She was still dating Lyle, but he was no longer a contender. Sophie, on the other hand, made it clear she had no interest in marriage, and was quite happy with her collection of younger trophy-boy escorts.

Jackie told them how Josh had helped her with the move and Sophie brought up birth control immediately. Even Isabel was a little taken aback by her friend's abruptness.

"I wouldn't consider having a physical relationship with Josh," Jackie defended him. "It would be considered statutory rape."

"True," Sophie agreed, "but regardless, if you have sex, you need to avoid an unwanted pregnancy."

"I'm well aware, but thank you," Jackie said. "I've been on birth control for the last year to control my acne."

"Acne?" Sophie inquired "Who told you you have acne?"

Jackie looked at her mother.

"You were breaking out," Isabel insisted.

"Well, it's working because your skin is perfectly clear." Sophie rolled her eyes at Isabel while Jackie was out of view.

Jackie was happy now that her mother had gotten her on the pill, because she was looking forward to the time when she would need it.

When they said their goodbyes and Jackie locked up for the night, she didn't feel lonely. She had a picture of her dad near her bed and she felt he was watching over her.

She wondered how Joanne was doing. She was no longer hurt by Joanne not recognizing or remembering her, but instead decided to be there for her when she needed her, as her dad would want. With Josh in her life, her improved relationship with her mother and now college starting, she wanted to be a resource for Joanne.

She would call Dr. Wright soon for an update, and find out how she could be of help.

CHAPTER FIFTY-TWO

Former Green Beret Rick Jones had been tracking Collins' movements on a daily basis and reporting them to Lou at regular intervals. Lou knew Jones through the bounty-hunter who worked for Vasquez.

The bounty-hunter—known only as Mr. X—told anyone who would listen, "You don't mess with Rick Jones."

Mr. X had escorted Collins to the Vasquez compound years earlier. Mr. X maintained loyalty to well paying clients, regardless of their loyalties, and he kept his emotions out of business. He asked only that his payment and whereabouts remain untraceable.

But Rick Jones' blood ran red, white and blue. He ran his own private investigation firm after retiring from 20 years in the military, and at the moment one of his firm's priorities was tracking the former reporter's activities in and around Hollywood landmarks.

The connections weren't revealing much so Jones added a second-in-command, Clark Roberts, to the Collins detail early on. This gave Jones the opportunity to take on a high profile politician's security detail for two weeks.

Jones was the epitome of a soldier. He was a 6' tall physically fit charmer who could extract information from just about anyone. His sandy hair was military short, cropped close to his skull, but long enough to run a comb through. His teeth were a brilliant white and his smile crooked slightly to his left. He wore khaki cargo pants, white t-shirts and black steel-toed boots most often, and a suit when absolutely necessary. He was a man of few words and, being single, he was free to travel as needed for assignments.

He was to keep eyes on Mark Collins 24/7, tracking his whereabouts and seeing that no harm came to Jackie or Isabel Manning. For that reason, he trusted his fellow Green Beret, Clark Roberts, a sniper who could hit a dollar bill at 1000 yards, to watch over Jackie.

Clark's backup, Dane Blacksmith watched Isabel and Bart Petty was on Collins. Blacksmith was a Special Ops retiree and Petty was a 20-year LAPD veteran.

The team was costing Lou Bartalow an enormous amount of money, but he could afford it. He was confident Collins was going to make a move on the Manning women and he was going to make damn sure the reporter was stopped in his tracks.

Lou's conscience was getting the best of him, so he went to Zach's grave to have a talk with his old friend. It pissed him off that Collins had seen through his veneer and knew what no one else did, that Lou worked every relationship to his own benefit and had no real friends.

"Guess you were my only real friend," Lou said as he poured a beer over Zach's grave. "I figured we'd both have a cold one."

Lou sat on the ground in a squat and his belly formed a round ball that protruded over his belt. He was uncomfortable, both physically and emotionally.

"So I'm going to come clean, man." Lou's eyes filled with tears, "I've called a lot of people friend, and most were business relationships or part of the Hollywood social hierarchy. But you, Herb Green and Jim Sikes are the only real friends I have. God, *had*. I've lost track of Sikes and Green. Well, I saw the Sikeses and their daughter, Marnie, at your wake, but I didn't even ask how to stay in touch. What kind of dick have I become?"

Lou took another beer off the six-pack ring. He flipped the tab and started to weep uncontrollably.

"I'm going to make this up to you, buddy." He took a long swig of beer. "I didn't forget."

He poured another beer over Zach's grave, then clinked the two beer cans together and tried to laugh, but started to cry again instead.

"We should have talked it out, man," Lou bellowed. "I just reacted and tried to fix the Collins problem. We should have talked, man!" Lou threw half a beer at Zach's headstone. "Fuck! Neither of us knew he'd come back."

Lou chucked both of the remaining beers at the headstone, one at a time. The second one burst and sprayed on him.

"Got me back." Lou laughed. "God, Joanne doesn't even know you're here…"

A groundskeeper approached Lou, but didn't get to speak before Lou retaliated.

"Don't fucking ask me if I'm okay. I'm not. I'm having a beer with my friend and if you don't give us some space, I'm going to fucking kill you."

"The sprinkler is coming on in a few," the young man said. "You're going to get wet. There are signs." He pointed to some signs posted on the grounds.

"So you don't care?" Lou was now feeling a buzz. He tried to get up on his knees and flopped back to his butt. "We have something in common, I'm a bastard, too."

"I'm not a bastard," the groundskeeper said. "And I'm sorry you and your friend didn't get to talk when he was alive."

"You're listening?" Lou was royally pissed. "Now I'm going to kill you."

"You are loud enough that anyone can hear you, sir."

"You should let the dead rest, brother. Don't respond." Lou shook his head, "Don't say another word. I'm trying to keep my cool."

The groundskeeper heard a hiss and moved quickly down a path and out of the line of the smelly reclaimed water.

"Son of a bitch," Lou screamed.

CHAPTER FIFTY-THREE

Marnie and Jackie were at Hollywood and Highland kicking around the idea of seeing a film at Mann's Chinese Theater. They were bored.

Marnie was also looking for a potential suitor, she informed Jackie.

"Halloween is a month away and I was thinking of finding a Manson look-a-like to be my date," Marnie laughed.

"Right," Jackie said. "Don't joke about something like that."

"I'm not joking," Marnie stopped. "Why can't you be a little more supportive?"

"I believe I have been," Jackie's eyes got big.

"What's that supposed to mean?"

"The whole Valley of the Dolls thing and the pill jar was okay. I thought you were just trying to be cool and mysterious in high school... but seriously, the Sharon Tate murder obsession is not funny."

"I'm not being funny, bitch." Marnie pinched Jackie's arm.

"Ouch. That was vicious," Jackie backed up.

"You're vicious. You think because you're sleeping with Josh, a male nurse, what a *joke*, that you're better than me?"

"I'm not sleeping with Josh and I don't think I'm better than you. You're living in a dream world!" Jackie walked away.

"Oh, like you're one to talk?" Marnie followed her. "You and your family's whole Marquel/Joanne baby-killer thing. Sharon was the victim... and her baby. Joanne is a walking time bomb and I heard she shot her first husband and left him in the woods."

Jackie's mouth dropped. It never dawned on her that Marnie was jealous of her. "Wow, you know... you know what we've been through. My father is dead!"

"Yeah, and I was more upset at the wake than you were," Marnie pinched Jackie again.

Jackie pinched Marnie back.

Marnie didn't flinch.

"You couldn't handle the stress I've been under, at least not without your pill collection!" Jackie snapped, truly hurt.

"See," Marnie pinched her again.

"Stop that or I am going to slap you." Jackie screamed.

Clark Roberts stopped about ten feet behind them and lit a cigarette. He grabbed a nearby bench and sat with his back to the young women, listening.

"It always comes back to you. I can't have a Manson look-a-like for a Halloween date because it might steal your thunder. You are a selfish bitch!" Marnie screamed back.

Souvenir shoppers were beginning to gather around them. A few vendors stepped out, and one suggested Marnie come in and look at the Sharon Tate posters.

Jackie didn't want to leave Marnie alone, but more for fear she might bring a crazy person back to their apartment.

"I apologize," Jackie didn't know why she was apologizing, but if it shut Marnie up, it would be worth it.

"For what?" Marnie probed.

Jackie had no idea how she would dig her way out of this. "I don't know, Marnie, I just apologize. I'm not trying to be the center of the universe."

"Wow," Marnie lit up again, "you never stop. I mean to actually admit that you think you are the center of the universe proves my point."

Jackie was numb. "I said I apologize."

A vendor came over and handed Marnie a poster, "Yours, it's Sharon Tate."

"Aww, that was so sweet, I will tell everyone how nice you are," she gushed, giving the Greek looking man a hug.

Jackie folded her arms and waited for the moment to pass. She caught her reflection and quickly put her arms down and held on to the strap of her purse.

It was all getting to be too much. Maybe she needed a shrink?

"Let's grab some lo mein and go back to the apartment, I want to hang this poster," Marnie squealed.

Lo mein sounded good. Jackie nodded. Maybe she was making too much of Marnie's quirks. Maybe she needed to lighten up and not be so serious.

Roberts followed them to the Chinese takeout and back to their apartment. They seemed to be settled for the evening.

Isabel was also in for the evening, Blacksmith reported. Jones and Petty were quiet.

CHAPTER FIFTY-FOUR

Today was the day, Collins decided.

He originally intended to confront Joanne during the seminar Q&A, rattle her and get under skin. From there he had a series of attacks planned for Isabel and Jackie that would disturb Zach, but with Zach gone it just pushed up the inevitable for Joanne.

Now it was too easy.

He didn't have to kidnap her and give her and Zach a taste of what he went through when he was first abducted and taken to Bogota.

She was a now willing participant. Adrian Jackson had truly given him a gift.

He got to the Wright/Goldberg residence a little before dusk. The women wouldn't be home yet and he and Joanne could take their time.

Joanne was out by the pool reading when he drove up.

She waved. He waved back.

As he approached, she got up and gave him a hug. "I've never been on a motorcycle."

She looped an arm in his and walked him to the guesthouse. "I'll need a jacket."

He almost liked her at this moment. She had never been remotely kind or considerate to him in the past. "I'll let you wear my helmet," Collins remarked. "I only have one."

"That's sweet of you," she smiled at him. "I'm going to leave a note."

Collins hadn't thought about her leaving a note, but it was a great way to frame Ken.

"I told Greta you were taking me to lunch a few days ago and you never showed up. She said to tell you hello."

"Really," Collins said. Then he remembered the message from Greta was intended for Ken, not him. "Just say in the note that they shouldn't wait up."

Joanne laughed. "They are a bit protective."

"Well they won't have to worry much longer."

Joanne ignored his comment and put her jacket on, then tried his helmet. "Take your protein pills and put your helmet on," Joanne sang. "Ground control to Major Ken."

He wondered how she could recall lyrics and not him.

"It's time to leave the capsule if you dare," Collins said. He refused to sing along with Joanne.

She saluted. "Roger that."

Rick Jones radioed to Clark Roberts. He wanted an update.

"Not much happening," Roberts replied. "I've been watching the kid and the mother's been shopping a lot, nothing to write home about. Jackie's roommate might be the most dangerous person in the equation."

"Where's Collins?" Jones asked.

"Sullivan Canyon, Petty says Collins is taking Joanne Manning on the bike."

"Christ," Jones said. "What's Petty driving?"

"His jeep," Roberts answered.

"I'm at a fundraiser, grab my bike at the office and hightail it to wherever Collins is taking Manning," Jones snapped the gum he was chewing.

His jaw was tight. Bartalow was right about Collins, but had the target all wrong. They needed to focus on Joanne Manning.

Josh and Jackie took a walk around the UCLA campus. It was a brisk night and a full moon. They made a plan to take it slow and do the simple things, like going to campus events, or a movie, grabbing a bite. There was no hurry, they were enjoying a true courtship.

Jackie stopped at a long set of steps and sat down on one. Josh joined her. They held each other and watched the scenery.

This was their routine. Just quiet times holding hands, cuddling or talking about silly things. He was the love she needed in her life. It was as though her father had gifted her Josh.

"Do you think I'm the one?" Jackie asked Josh.

Josh kissed her forehead. "Maybe I should ask you the same thing."

They didn't say a word. They gazed into each other's eyes and gave in to the kiss that they were both feeling.

Collins was hungry and in no rush. They definitely had time to grab a bite.

At a traffic light he asked Joanne, "If you could have only one meal, what would you choose?"

"Surf and turf, of course. How about you?"

Of course, he thought. Well, she would be paying him back soon enough… "Pot roast with oven brown potatoes like my mother used to make." He could almost taste it.

"That sounds good." Joanne said above the traffic.

A jeep moved up beside them, followed by a black SUV.

"Well, I've got a place for your steak." Traffic was starting to move.

"Ok," she yelled.

The jeep kept pace with them and hung back as they approached The Palm in West Hollywood. Collins didn't much care if they were spotted together. Most people didn't approach celebrities, they just pointed and whispered, or snapped pictures. Besides, anything that might be published would just tick up his book sales. His publisher wanted a follow up and boy did he have one planned!

They both ate too much.

Collins walked past the bar on his way to the restroom and saw a man that looked oddly like a member of the cartel. It spooked him. He was certain it was a coincidence, but just to be sure he decided to get the hell out of there.

"Let's head out."

"No dessert?" She laughed. "I know. I couldn't eat another bite. Let's have a coffee and just kill time and relax."

"Kill time and relax," Collins echoed. He threw some cash down and she got up and begrudgingly followed him.

A girl at the door pointed to them.

Collins walked behind Joanne and said, "Ignore them."

"I love you Joanne," the girl said. "Can I get an autograph."

"No," Collins gave the girl a stern look.

"Oh my, you are…"

He pushed Joanne out the door before she could hear much else.

Dr. Wright picked up her den phone and propped up her feet. "Oh, hello Ken, how is it going?"

"Fine," Ken answered. "Evan and I were thinking and we would like to have you all over for dinner tomorrow."

"Two nights in row? Well, you two are really catching up. I'll check with Greta if you want to hold."

"Two nights?" Ken repeated. He clasped his hand over the mouthpiece and whispered to Evan, "I think Judith is showing her age, she just said two nights…"

Greta picked up the phone. "We'd love dinner, Ken. Tell Joanne it's fine with us if it's fine with her."

Ken covered the mouthpiece and whispered to Evan, "I think it's catching." He cleared his throat and said to Greta, "Well, we thought you three would discuss it and get back to us."

"We're okay and if Joanne's okay, it's a date. What should we bring?"

Ken mouthed to Evan, 'I think they are drinking.'

"A salad and a red table wine okay?" Greta asked.

"Sounds good." Ken replied. "We're hoping Joanne'll be in better spirits this time."

"What happened?" Greta was concerned.

"I beg your pardon?" Ken was shaking his head.

"Aren't you at dinner?"

"We're talking about dinner tomorrow…" Ken said.

"No I'm talking about now."

"Greta, are you smoking weed? You're making no sense."

"Ken, she IS with you?"

"Joanne? I think I'd know if she were with me." Ken shook his head.

"She left a note. She was going for a ride on your motorcycle…" Greta realized what she was saying.

"We haven't seen her since the hospital." Ken was super confused.

"Shit!" Greta said.

"What? Speak English."

"Joanne is gone … with somebody who claims to be you!"

"Claims to be…"

"She left a note… I didn't think you rode a motorcycle."

"Jesus Greta, do I look like someone who would risk his life in LA traffic on two wheels?" Ken was perturbed, "Who would pretend to…? Oh, fuck. Collins!"

Lou Bartalow was alerted to Joanne's dinner with Collins. Jones reassured him he had a man keeping pace with the two.

Dane Blacksmith stayed on Isabel's home, but Clark Roberts had to leave Jackie's and grab Jones' chopper to meet Bart Petty, who was still following the couple in his jeep.

A black tie political fundraiser kept Rick Jones and a newer hire busy, but he was able to see Bartalow at the event.

Bartalow was alone, but doing his part to support the candidate who would vote on legislation that would continue to keep his investments growing. He was surprised to see Jones, but also glad to get an update on the Manning women's safety.

"Where are they?" Bartalow whispered to Jones, referring to Collins and Joanne.

"Near the Griffith Park Observatory," Jones kept his eyes forward as he spoke to Bartalow.

"Are you going to stop them?" Lou asked.

"They had dinner and are taking a drive, that is all we've observed. There are no signs of distress and it would be premature to make contact," Jones said. "Now if you'll excuse me..." He moved toward the politician's table.

Isabel phoned Jackie and got a busy signal. She wasn't comfortable knowing that Marnie was using drugs and she feared Jackie might become attracted to recreational use herself. UCLA wasn't a great distance away, but she knew she had to trust Jackie.

Lyle slapped Isabel on the ass. "Why are you calling Jackie now?"

Isabel rolled onto her back and pulled the covers up over her bare breasts. "I don't know. I'm just concerned."

"She's fine. She's probably doing what we're doing," he laughed.

"I think I'd be less concerned if she were." Isabel stroked Lyle's chest, "It's Marnie that worries me."

"Since when do you worry? They've been friends for years, Isabel. It's not like they haven't had parties and opportunities to get into trouble before now."

"I guess Zach's death and Jackie moving out have made me vulnerable," Isabel muttered.

"Vulnerable?" Lyle said as he began to kiss her. "It's a control issue, plain and simple."

"Perhaps..."

"And now it's time for you to lose control." He moved down to her breasts.

"Lyle!" Isabel purred.

CHAPTER FIFTY-FIVE

"The sky is gorgeous," Joanne yelled above the wind and the sound of the motorcycle. She leaned in and held on tightly.

It seemed Ken was going faster than necessary and she couldn't understand why he swerved through traffic so erratically. She figured he was trying to impress her.

They were now moving too fast for the twists and turns of Beachwood Drive and she held him even tighter.

"We're going there," Collins pointed to the Hollywood sign.

"How exciting!" Joanne shouted.

Roberts radioed Petty before he mounted the chopper. "What's your location?"

"I lost them, I'm stuck on the 101. I watched with my binoculars as far as I could and it looked like they were heading toward Griffith Park. They also could have turned around by now, who the hell knows?" Petty was pissed.

Roberts started the Harley. "Sounds like they're headed to Mt. Lee."

"As good a guess as any." Petty hung his head out the window, "Jesus Christ would you fucking move!"

Roberts was surprised by his colleague's short fuse. "Petty man, the road rage is not going to help anything."

Petty laid on his horn, "Move your motherfucking cars!" He realized Roberts was talking to him. "Sorry, what?"

"I'll catch you later." Roberts signed off.

Jones caught Bartalow on his way to the valet. "We lost Collins. My men believe they know where he is. They believe he is headed to Mt. Lee."

Lou shook his head, "The Hollywood Sign?"

"Appears to be."

"You don't think they're going to screw or something? I mean, Jesus, maybe this whole chase is nuts," Lou wanted some guidance.

"It's a moonlit night." Jones snapped his gum. "You hired me. What are we doing?"

"I don't fucking know." Lou was agitated.

"Then we'll find them and report back," Jones gave Bartalow one slap to the middle of the back and moved into position as the political entourage made their exit.

Collins rolled the motorcycle to a spot that would be shadowed if another vehicle approached.

Joanne stretched her legs and warmed her hands together. "The sky is gorgeous."

"I'm going to take a piss. Then we're going to take a little hike and see if we can jog your memory," Collins said.

He didn't wait for a reply, moving instead into the shadows to relieve himself. The release felt good. Now he could focus on her.

He walked her to the edge of a scenic overlook. "Do you know why I brought you here?"

"To see this marvelous landmark and the city lights?"

"That's a perk."

"No clue," Joanne rubbed her nose. It was cold and running.

"That always seems to be the case with you, doesn't it? But now it's time get down to business." His tone and demeanor had changed.

Even in the dark she could see his expression was menacing.

"Ken, you sound angry," Joanne stayed calm. "You're scaring me."

"I am angry, Joanne. And I'm not Ken Avery." Collins grabbed both sides of her jacket collar and stared at her. He had so many things going through his mind. She had no idea what scared meant.

"Who are you?"

"Mark Collins, remember?" He pulled her closer.

"No." She shivered. "I don't..."

She tried to pull away, but he held her tight.

"We're taking a hike." He pulled a shiny object from his pants, snapping one handcuff to her wrist and the other on his.

Roberts pulled off at Deronda and got out his night vision binoculars. He had to avoid looking into the light of the Hollywood letters as they would blind his vision. He wanted to see if he could spot any activity near the landmark, but all he found were a couple of coyotes.

He took out his range finder to see what the distance was to the sign—about 366 meters out. It was a crisp night and there wasn't much wind. He still wasn't certain Collins and Joanne had gone in this direction, it was just a feeling.

He radioed Petty only to learn Petty hadn't progressed much and was looking for a spot to hit the 4-wheel drive and cut a path off the 101.

"I'm not seeing anything," Roberts reported to Petty. "I'm going to hang back and survey the scene."

He rode a short distance to a spot off Mulholland Highway where an open lot with a slight elevation provided him a place to dig in and observe.

The full moon wasn't helping. He was exposed by the bright night sky. The foliage on the terrain was dark and the sky over Mt. Lee was bright.

Then he saw what looked like two individuals struggling on the slope near the D.

"I have visual. The subjects are moving east to west," Roberts radioed Petty.

Then he heard Petty lay on his horn.

Ken and Evan paced their home. They weren't certain if they should head to Dr. Wright's or call the police. But it wasn't their place to call the LAPD, Joanne wasn't their guest and they barely knew the circumstances surrounding her disappearance or rendezvous with Collins.

It was clear Collins duped Joanne into believing he was Ken, who else could it be? "I need another drink, Ev." Ken grabbed for the good scotch.

"You've got to slow down." Evan poured a small amount into Ken's glass for him.

"Jesus, what if someone really thinks I abducted her…"

"It's clear you have an alibi," Evan said. "She's the one at risk, not you."

Ken slugged the scotch.

"You're moving too fast," Joanne screamed. "We're going to fall to our death!"

Collins yanked her hard. "Do you think this is some sort of field trip?"

She cried. "Why are so angry with me?"

"Just keep your fucking mouth shut and follow me." He yanked again at the cuffed hand and her feet slid. She screamed and grabbed onto Collins. He managed to steady himself and keep her from pulling them both down the mountain.

"You're hurting me." Joanne cried. "I'm cooperating. Please, I'm cooperating."

Isabel and Lyle were both snoring when the bedroom door opened. Two individuals entered on their bellies and moved items around in the room, clearly looking for something.

Isabel stirred and told Lyle she was going to go to the bathroom.

She didn't bother dressing, she got up and walked across to the room to the bathroom. She didn't turn on the lights or close the bathroom door. She just sat on the toilet and placed her face in her palms and urinated.

Once she was done, she rinsed her hands in the sink and got back in bed. She almost stepped on one of the intruders as she pushed the bedroom door closed. She couldn't remember it being open.

She nuzzled close to Lyle and asked him if he had gotten up for a glass of water.

Lyle continued to snore. She went back to sleep.

Dane Blacksmith spotted what appeared to be two people in dark clothing exiting Isabel Manning's home. One crouched down near the front window when the security lights came on.

The other appeared unsteady and struggled to stay vertical.

"I have two suspects at the Isabel Manning residence." Blacksmith radioed Jones. He had no clue when or how they got in. "Jesus, I'm going in."

"Get Petty if needed. Roberts has visual on Collins," Jones was short.

The political function was over and the proximity to Mt. Lee was close enough that Jones could meet up with Roberts within minutes.

He was now concerned that there was a coordinated attack in place and he needed to get a man back at Jackie's. The new hire would follow the politician until he was safely home and Petty was being rerouted to Jackie's apartment.

"LAPD just arrived," Blacksmith said to a dead radio. "Did you call them?"

He realized Jones hadn't heard him. He chucked the radio to his passenger seat.

"Here we are," Collins seemed pleased with himself.

They were standing under the towering H.

"This is where we will say our goodbyes." He took the key out of his pocket and unlocked the handcuffs.

Joanne didn't say a word. She began to rub the sore wrist, not certain what would happen next.

Without warning Collins shoved Joanne to ground as hard as he could. The force pushed her tailbone first to the ground and she saw the tremendous light from the sign above her as her head hit the rough terrain. She lost her breath and was gasping for air.

"It will all be over soon." Collins pulled out the pocket knife he had used on his own pinkie finger.

He knelt down and smacked her face hard.

"Breathe dammit." He shook her and she started to gasp. He let her head fall to the dirt.

Collins held the knife next to her neck so she wouldn't move.

"See this cut," he showed her his pinkie, "I almost sawed it off with this knife. It's razor sharp, so if you decide to sit up suddenly, you'll slit your own throat."

She was dazed and confused. She had an odd sensation looking up at the sky and the sign lights. It was like déjà vu. Where had she been or what had she done...? Collins was rattling on about his imprisonment in Bogotá and she couldn't put any of his words together.

"Did you know," Collins asked, "that a young actress hung herself from the H, well not that exact H, but the original Hollywoodland H. Her name was Peg Entwistle. She's known for her death more than her life."

Joanne said nothing, her eyes grew larger.

"I so preferred you when you were Marquel, at least you stood up for yourself. As Joanne, you're such a huge bore."

She was remembering the stage and the lights from the seminar.

"The followup to Joanne's Story has to have a literal Hollywood ending…"

"What would Marquel do?" Joanne was still feeling foggy from the head injury.

"She would never have gotten on the motorcycle," Collins laughed at her.

Joanne now remembered speaking on the seminar stage and the voices… she moved her hand over her abdomen. The wounds had healed, but she was remembering.

Without warning a shot rang out and Collins fell back beside her, the knife flying out of his hand. He screamed, "My shoulder… Christ!"

The sound of the shot echoed in her ears. Joanne screamed and curled up, fully expecting to be the next one hit.

Collins tried to sit up and felt faint. "Bitch! Christ, I'm bleeding."

Joanne started to crawl away from Collins and he grabbed her ankle with his right hand. "You're not…"

She made a fist and punched Collins in the groin. He struggled for breath.

A bullhorn called out, "Are you safe?"

Joanne wasn't certain who was calling out, or where they were.

"We're here to help you." The voice boomed.

The full moon was bright, but she couldn't see where the voice was coming from. She crawled upward as she was too afraid to stand. She was sure she'd fall down the slope.

Collins rocked back and forth, holding his balls with his right hand.

"We're coming down. Just hang tight."

Roberts radioed Petty. "Are you at Mt. Lee?"

Petty didn't answer.

Roberts could see activity north of Collins and Joanne. He shot Collins in the shoulder when he saw the knife glinting and confirmed that he intended personal harm to Joanne. He could see in his night vision that Joanne was now moving away from Collins.

CHAPTER FIFTY-SIX

Joanne got to the top of Mt. Lee and heard a gun cock.

She froze. A black SUV was parked nearby but she couldn't see who was watching her.

"We're going to protect you," the Spanish accent conveyed.

"Not so fast," another voice said and another gun cocked.

"I'm not the one you want." Her voice was quavering, "The man who was trying to hurt me is down there."

"We are hoisting him up," the Spanish voice said. "You need not worry Marquel."

A rough baritone voice declared, "Humberto Vasquez your ass is mine. You're wanted for human trafficking and drug trafficking."

A third voice moved out of the shadows and said, "X, that you?" Rick Jones stepped up beside Mr. X and trained his weapon on Vasquez.

Joanne collapsed.

Mr. X looked at Jones, "I just want the bounty on Vasquez, you can deal with the woman and the reporter."

Vasquez refused to drop his weapon. "X, we've paid you well on the jobs you've done for us. What do you want? I've got more money than any bounty you'll receive on me."

Mr. X ignored the Colombian.

Vasquez addressed Jones. "I want the woman, she's a goddess to my family. I'll take the reporter off your hands, too."

"I'm here for the woman and the reporter, Vasquez," Jones chimed in snapping his gum.

"What's your price? You both can retire together?" Vasquez quipped at Mr. X and Rick Jones.

Collins wailed in the background as Vasquez's thugs put a black sack over his head, "Somebody kill me, please. I'm not going back to Bogota."

"I'm insulted Collins, you were well treated, like a brother," Vasquez said loudly.

Each man stood firm and kept their weapons in place. Rick Jones or Mr. X could take Vasquez down.

"Vasquez, you're not taking Joanne Manning for a sex slave!" Jones boomed.

"Jesus, no!" Vasquez said. "She's going to be my bride. The pride of my family. We all love Marquel."

Collins struggled, but couldn't get out of the grips of the Colombians. "Humberto," Collins said. "I know that voice. He's the one who originally abducted me! Humberto, he's working you!"

"That's my brother, Collins!" Vasquez said. "Yes, we hired X to bring you to Colombia, were you not listening? I do appreciate that you are loyal to me, Collins, and I will bring you back to Bogota where you belong."

"No, no, no. I'm… staying in the states. NO!" Collins shouted.

Joanne stirred.

Vasquez' thugs dropped Collins and trained their weapons on Jones and X.

"Let's do this!" One of the younger thugs said to Vasquez.

An LAPD helicopter rose above them, shining its spotlight over the mountainside. The speaker from the chopper boomed above them. "Give up your weapons and this will end peacefully." An officer clearly had a weapon trained on Humberto.

Joanne could feel the bright light through her eyelids. She didn't want to open her eyes. She heard the exchanges and she prayed that however this ended, she would die.

She understood that she had survived the loss of her daughter, Marquel, and her first husband George. She wasn't certain where Zach was, but she didn't think he was looking for her. Something was wrong. She wanted Zach to rescue her. She desperately wanted to see him and hear his voice, but she knew he wasn't coming. She let out a gasp and began to cry.

Jones chewed his gum hard and glanced briefly at the woman, feeling a tug in his heart. He wondered how one person could survive so much pain. There was no way he was going to let her suffer further, not on his watch.

"What are you going to do Vasquez?" Jones asked.

"I've got good lawyers... plenty of money to fight any charge..." He dropped his weapon. "Take care of him," he shouted to his thugs.

They nodded to each other as though they already had it planned. One shot Collins in the head and the other shot Mr. X in the heart. Simultaneously Jones took out the thug to his right and the officer in the helicopter took down the one on his left.

The only two left standing were Jones and Vasquez, with Joanne still whimpering on ground in a fetal position.

"Keep your eyes closed, Ms. Manning," Jones said, training his gun on Vasquez again.

A motorcycle could be heard ascending the mountain. Roberts waved to Jones, parked the cycle and apprehended Vasquez, holding him until the LAPD ground unit arrived.

Jones picked up Joanne and again encouraged her to keep her eyes closed. She held onto him tightly. He wanted to shield her from the crime scene. He noticed the SUV. His jeep was open to the elements and at least the SUV could provide cover. He nodded to Roberts, who jogged over and opened the black van. Roberts looked inside and waved off Jones.

Roberts was shocked to find three young women inside, tied, gagged and drugged.

"The jeep," he told Jones.

"Joanne," Jones said. "You're safe now."

Joanne opened her eyes to see Rick Jones' faint smile as he sat her on the passenger seat.

Her face was smudged and scratched from her struggles with Collins.

"Thank you," she whispered.

"You'll be needed for questioning," Jones said. "But I'll see to it that you're protected."

Blacksmith radioed Jones.

"Isabel Manning and her male companion are safe."

"What happened?" Jones demanded. He walked away from the vehicle so Joanne couldn't hear.

"Marnie Sikes got into the house earlier in the day via the maid. She watched the maid plug in the security code and came back later with a homeless man while Manning and Herlbert were asleep. Claims she was attempting a Manson-style creepy-crawly mission. She said it was a joke and Jackie knew about it. Her father's on his way to post bail," Blacksmith said.

"What about Jackie?" Jones asked.

"She's safe."

Jones looked at Joanne. She had a far off look, but a serene look.

CHAPTER FIFTY-SEVEN

Sophie Krentz had Isabel and Lyle over for cocktails so she could hear all the gossip about the HOLLYWOOD Sign Massacre. She wanted the dirt from the best sources possible.

"Where do I begin?" Isabel asked. She patted Lyle's hand with her left. They had finally come to terms and he had placed a big shiny rock on her engagement finger. They were going to have a big wedding and hopefully grow his law practice.

Isabel was being brought on as a partner to lure celebrity clients into the fold. The stipulation being that client confidentially was priority one and any breach would void their agreement.

"Let me say this much, Marnie Sikes will no longer room with Jackie!" Isabel said.

"What has Marnie done?"

"It never hit the media, but she was attempting a creepy-crawly at my house when we were sleeping." She shook her head, remembering the events of that night, "She had a homeless man with her. God only knows how long they were in the house! "

"Little Marnie?"

"Spoiled brat, bitch," Isabel said. "She's on drugs, too."

"What does Jackie say?"

"She's relieved that we're okay and is well aware that Marnie needs professional help. Once they started rooming together, she wasn't sure how to get rid of Marnie."

"Where is she now?" Sophie pulled her scarf up around her chins, an unconscious habit.

"Her parents sent her off to some spa in Mexico to get her head together."

"Like that's going to do any good," Sophie shook the martini shaker and poured herself another drink. "Was the Manson thing part of a hazing? I mean, how would she or Jackie know anything about 1969? They weren't even born."

"It's a long story," Isabel began.

"Do tell," Sophie said.

Lyle squeezed Isabel's hand. He wanted to change topics.

"Maybe Jackie will tell you someday." Isabel looked at her ring. She was in love with it, and the accomplishment it represented.

"Careful," Sophie said, "that thing might blind you."

"What?" Isabel asked absently.

"You did well, Lyle," Sophie winked and sipped her martini. "She can't stop looking at the damn thing."

Isabel was a little embarrassed and laughed. "Guilty."

"So what's the dirt on Joanne?" Sophie was anxious.

"Pursuit published an article that Joanne begged Collins to help her end her life under the H of the Hollywood sign. That she wanted to be the next Peggy Entwistle."

"I saw that," Sophie waved dismissively. "Why was Humberto Vasquez after Collins?"

"I think Collins and Humberto were lovers, but Vasquez and most of Colombia are addicted to Suburban Life reruns… and Humberto was supposedly in love with Marquel…" Isabel shrugged. "Who knows?"

"Oh!" Sophie said, "I get it. The Marquel story is like a Spanish soap opera, only way more intriguing. That's why they're interested!"

"You are stereotyping the good people of Colombia," Lyle said.

"So I am," Sophie admitted. "But I get it."

Isabel offered to make another round of martinis, but Lyle got up to make them.

"But why did Vasquez have Collins killed?" Sophie asked.

"Lyle opened a new bottle of vodka, "He wasn't a free man to Humberto. His men followed Collins as early as the seminar where Joanne was shot."

"Is this fact or a theory?" Sophie queried.

"I know someone who knows someone, and Vasquez was tailing Collins and Joanne, hoping to abscond with them both at the same venue. They were all caught off guard by the shooter, Jackson."

"Your source knows this how...?" Isabel asked.

"Knowledgeable connections," Lyle shook the martini shaker. He would say no more.

"I liked Collins, the poor bastard." Sophie added, "I mean he was a great reporter. He did uncover Joanne's—or Marquel's—identity. You have to give him that."

Isabel's mouth dropped. "Sophie! He was stalking me and we learned that he was renting a house a few blocks…"

Sophie's eyes lit up. "Oh my God, didn't the homeowner's association fight to keep the address from being released?"

"I wouldn't doubt it," Isabel said.

Lyle laughed.

"Poor Collins," Sophie was still defending the reporter who used to attend her parties. "He was one troubled man. Did you see the elaborate collage of photos he had plastered around the rental house? There was a full spread in the Sunday Times."

Lyle sat next to Isabel and placed his hand on her thigh. Isabel looked up and gave him a kiss.

"You two are seriously making me sick," Sophie slugged her drink.

"Soph!" Lyle was surprised.

"It's like you both have seen each other for the first time."

"You're such a romantic," Isabel said.

"We're all adults. But seriously, you two have to stop touching each other, it's just unnatural."

Dr. Wright and Greta welcomed Joanne home to their guesthouse. Joanne agreed to stay for a short time. She wanted to get reacquainted with Jackie and return to the home she had made with Zach.

She understood what had happened during her speaking engagement, and Zach's heart attack. She was in denial of her feelings. She knew she would need the doctor's help to heal.

Jackie was nervous as Josh brought her to Dr. Wright's home. She had not seen Joanne since the hospital. Jackie and Josh sat poolside and waited for Joanne to come out of the guesthouse.

Dr. Wright, Greta and Rick Jones were in the kitchen of the main home. Jones was hired by Joanne as a bodyguard, but at the moment he was giving her a chance to be alone. The doctor and Greta were preparing snacks for Joanne's guests.

Joanne watched from her doorway and saw Jackie holding Josh's hand. Her eyes welled with tears. She knew Zach would be so proud of the woman Jackie had become and she couldn't help thinking of her own daughter, Marquel. How would she have looked at this age? There was joy and pain in her thoughts.

She had to get out there, there was no reason to keep waiting. Joanne slid the glass door open and stepped out, barefoot. They didn't notice until she was just a few feet away from them.

She smiled at Jackie and began to cry.

Jackie and Josh both stood. Jackie hugged Joanne and they both wept. Josh excused himself.

"I missed you," Jackie said.

Joanne nodded. She felt a lump rise in her throat that wouldn't allow speech.

"Daddy fought hard. He loved you so."

Joanne held Jackie tighter.

"I miss my daughter when I see you," Joanne said. "I know you miss Zach, and I miss him too. So much..."

This was harder than Jackie realized; she wished her dad could be with them at this moment and make everything right. "I'm... your...family, Joanne," Jackie managed. "You're my step-mom."

Joanne smiled through the ache, "Thank you, Jackie. You're my reason to live."

Jackie's eyes got big. She wasn't expecting to hear anything like this. "Daddy wouldn't want you to ever be alone or afraid."

Joanne nodded.

"He did everything to protect you." Jackie rubbed her eyes.

Joanne stroked Jackie's hair. "It was his downfall."

Jackie was hurt. "Don't say it like that."

"It's okay, Jackie," Joanne reassured her. "He would want us to be honest."

"But it sounds so bad." Jackie pulled away.

"Please sit." Joanne encouraged.

They both sat down on the patio chairs. Joanne took Jackie's hands, wanting to clear the air. It was the only way she could resolve losing Zach.

"Your father and Lou Bartalow both apologized to me not long before the seminar. I just couldn't understand their guilt, but it was Lou's guilt that saved me. He hired Rick Jones to protect you, me and your mother."

Jackie hadn't heard this before. "The man who saved you … was protecting all of us?"

Joanne nodded.

"Lou hired Rick. Lou said he felt guilty after your father died and the only way to make it up to your dad was to hire someone to protect us."

"But why would he feel guilty and why was daddy apologizing?"

Joanne took a deep breath. "Lou and your father had Mark Collins sent to Bogota, Colombia after Collins broke the story of my identity."

"Daddy was just trying to protect you," Jackie defended.

"Your father didn't know what he was getting involved with and neither did Lou, until Carlos Vasquez died."

"Who is Carlos Vasquez?" Jackie asked.

"He was a very dangerous man who ran a drug cartel. He was involved in human trafficking of young women, many your age."

"Oh my God!" Jackie was shocked.

"Collins was allowed to leave Colombia after Carlos Vasquez died. It was Humberto Vasquez, the son of Carlos, who set a trap to capture me along with Collins."

Jackie's eyes got bigger. "But why?"

"It's a little crazy. They still think of me in Colombia as the actress Marquel."

"What?"

"Some people there have mixed my television identity and the Collins story about me... and they think I'm some kind of saint of broken hearts." Joanne looked away, embarrassed.

"Wouldn't they understand that you don't want to be forced to come to their country?" Jackie asked.

"It's not the Colombian people, it was just some power hungry drug lords who were behind my abduction plot."

Rick Jones came out to the patio and knelt next to Joanne. He introduced himself to Jackie.

"Let's continue inside... there will be plenty of time to catch up." He led the women into the main house.

EPILOGUE

Collins' book "Joanne's Story" stayed on the bestseller list for six months after the reporter's death. The Vasquez "autobiography" stayed on the bestseller list for a year longer as the trial of Humberto Vasquez was tied up in the US court system.

In time Jackie shared the funeral photos with Joanne.

Joanne moved back into her home and Rick Jones moved in to provide protection.

Ken signed on as Joanne's agent for publicity after Joanne created the Marquel Foundation to help find missing and exploited women and children. It was an irony of sorts, given that Joanne feared she might be exploiting her deceased child's name again, but she knew of no other name that would carry the weight needed to get serious legislation and backing.

She also needed to honor her daughter in some way, as Hollywood would never let her forget that she took her three-year-old's name when she became an actress.

Joanne had done so unconsciously, to give her child another chance to live.

Joanne believed that she could channel her loss into a charity that could save others.

Why else she was still alive?

ACKNOWLEDGEMENTS

My greatest fear is that I will forget to mention someone who has been an important part of this journey.

First, I'd like to thank my sister Ellen Williams for being a great editor. I am so blessed to have you in my life. I am especially grateful for the editing collaboration on this book. I trust Ellen completely. She is a gifted writer and understands how to work with my words, quirks and characters to make them shine. We bonded over many characters in this story and that brings me joy.

To Judy Roe, who is a former teacher colleague of my husband, Tom. Judy read the first book Marquel many years ago. When we reconnected at a dinner, Judy said, "when are you going to write another novel? You are one of my favorite authors."

Judy's words were so sincere that it truly changed my life. She was the first known fan of Marquel. Others came later, Robyn Fairbanks, Roxanne Holichork Smith, Roberta Terranova, Kim Salter and more.

To Lani Skuthorpe who I met through Bunny Cates on Twitter, Lani lives in Australia. I am just thrilled to connect with readers around the world. Lani enjoyed the first book Marquel and beta read the final draft of Marquel's Dilemma prior to editing. Her feedback helped me tremendously!! She is a Team George fan from the first book and I have promised Lani that she'll understand him better in the forthcoming Marquel's Redemption. Thanks Lani and Bunny!

Being an author is a lonely business and when someone takes the time to share this with you, it makes all the hard work worthwhile. I just can't thank my readers enough. It is a pleasure to share my characters and their adventures with you.

For the book reviewers and bloggers, God bless you! Sharing is caring and the time you take to help authors is immeasurable. A big shout out to Suleika Santana of All About Books or https://www.facebook.com/bookninjas2 and Michelle Bowman of WLK Book Promotions http://www.wlkbookpromotions.com.

To Lisa Despain of Ebookconverting.com, you make my life so much easier with the assistance in cover design and book formatting. You make me look good. Thanks Lisa.

To Robert Enriquez and our daughters Marquel Skinner and Blair Skinner, for the Marquel book trailer you made, it is amazing! I hope more people will watch it. Robert inspired me to write a film script for Marquel and it is currently in revision. Watch for a Kickstarter link for the film on my website: www.emilyskinnerbooks.com.

To my mother Barbara Williams, thanks for coming up with the title Marquel's Dilemma. To my husband Tom Skinner, thanks for being my best friend. I love you.

Other Works by Emily W. Skinner

Novels by Emily W. Skinner

Marquel

Marquel's Dilemma

Marquel's Redemption—coming soon

Booktrailer:
Marquel book trailer on YouTube—
featuring actor Eric Roberts & Marquel Skinner
www.youtube.com/watch?v=6e6O7iYqeVQ

Young Adult Novels by E. W. Skinner

St. Blair: Children of the Night Vol. 1

St. Blair: Children of the Night Vol. 2—coming soon

Sybille's Reign

Diary of St. Blair—coming soon

Sign up for email updates at:

www.emilyskinnerbooks.com

Follow Emily on:

www.facebook.com/emilyskinnerbooks

www.twitter.com/emilyauthor

http://www.thefilmmom.blogspot.com/

https://www.goodreads.com/author/show/
6982753.Emily_W_Skinner

ABOUT THE AUTHOR

Emily Skinner lives in Tampa Bay, Florida with her husband, Tom. In addition to writing, she also enjoys selling advertising, antiquing, and working with their daughters, Marquel Skinner and Blair Skinner on their film and acting projects.